Acting Monologues &
Scenes For Kids!

*Original Monologues and
Scenes For Kids
6 to 13...Combined Into One
Very Special Book!*

by Bo Kane

"Acting Monologues & Scenes For Kids!"
Revised Edition April 2023
Burbank Publishing
212 S. Reese Pl.
Burbank, California 91506
Burbankpublishing@gmail.com

ISBN 0-9841950-6-8

Written, published, and printed in the United States.
© 2020 Burbank Publishing   First Printing May 2020

Cover - Film Strip: Tyler/Tony. Makena/Fionn.
Nick/ Mylo/Tiber. Isa/Kendra. Jett/Raquel.
Trevor/Austin. Ruben. Lela/Victoria.
Scarlett/Dylan/Eddie.

Group: Sara, Jude, Samantha, Lucas, Scarlett,
Ayn, Bo, Eddie, Aristotle, Aiden, Tiber.
Book Cover and masks designed by **Thomas Cain**

For Denise, Makena, and Austin

The best job I've ever had, the best thing anyone has ever called me, is *'Dad'*. This book is dedicated to my wonderful wife and kids with all my love, admiration and respect.

*"Courage is being scared to death,
but saddling up anyway."*
- John Wayne

Monologues

Monologues

Acting Scenes

Acting Scenes

Scenes with an Adult

"Shorty" Scenes   *just a few lines each*

Everybody Acts

So, you want to act? Great! It takes a lot of bravery to put yourself in someone else's shoes and perform in front of an audience or camera. And, it takes a lot of practice. An actor prepares the same way a musician or athlete does. So, this book can be like your batting cage or music sheet…a way to practice your craft.

Some of us may end up acting professionally in movies, television, or on stage. Some of us may act just to make people laugh. It's fun, and it will help you be more at ease with your friends, teachers and classmates.

Shakespeare once wrote: *"All the world's a stage, and all the men and women merely players. They have their exits and their entrances; and one man in his time plays many parts."*

Many parts. So whether you become a professional actor ... or a teacher, doctor, chef, policeman or fashion designer ... **everybody acts.**

Foreword

This book is divided into four parts: acting by yourself (monologues), acting in a scene with someone near your age, acting with an adult, and "shorty scenes" –quick scenes with just a few lines each.

There are also **"Notes From The Coach"** sprinkled throughout the book. These are suggestions, questions or ideas about the characters/scenes for you to consider. You can use them or not, I won't take offense if you don't. (Well…maybe a little, but I'll get over it.)

The pieces are not divided up by age or gender; you will find your level and what works best for you, and that level will change over time. The short scenes are in the back of the book.

Most of the monologues and scenes can be played by either a boy or a girl, with just a minor adjustment or two. Not all---a few, such as "If I Only Had A Brain," are for a girl, and "Football For Real" is for boys.

For the **Monologues**, it's usually obvious who you're talking to; other times you have to pick someone, and it's important to put yourself in your character's shoes. How do

they feel? What happened just before?
What does your character want?

Same for the **Scenes,** and it's very important
to LISTEN to what the other character is
saying. And to *listen as your character
listens:* **hearing it for the very first time.**
Every time. And sometimes you have to
take your time; there are no prizes for
finishing the fastest.

Re-acting is essential. Play the "pauses". A
great actor acts, reacts and interacts.

Another point -- last one, I promise: there is
a different dynamic when the scene is
between a brother and sister, as opposed to a
boy and a girl from school. Our tone is
different when speaking to a sibling, and
that relationship can change our entire
character and the way he or she speaks.

Ok. Let's do it. And have some fun.

"When actors are talking, they are the
servants of the dramatist. It is what they can show
the audience when they are **not** talking that reveals
the fine actor."
                                        -Cedric Hardwicke

MONOLOGUES

mon uh lawg - *noun*
a part of a drama, or comedic solo,
in which a single actor speaks alone;
soliloquy.

"Play Outside"

QUINN is holding a microphone doing a
news report for The Kids' Health Network.

QUINN

Hi. This is Quinn Smith reporting for
'The Kids' Health Network'.
Most doctors agree that we need sixty
minutes of physical activity every
day. A full hour. And they mean
actual activity, not just playing video
games.
Playing outside helps build strong
muscles and bones, keeps your body
lean, and it's fun.
So if you want to live a long and
happy life, you have to exercise more
than just your thumbs. Get outside
and play!
This is Quinn Smith reporting for The
Kids' Health Network. Now back to
you in the studio.

"Butter-Fly"

A butterfly flies to a picnic table and lands
as KELLY approaches with a jar…

KELLY

Stay still, stay …. gotcha!
(the lid goes on the jar)
There you are; wow, you're beautiful.
Hey, take it easy! You'll hurt your
wings. Look, I put holes in the top so
you can breathe.   And some grass in
the bottom, too. Just like home.
(the butterfly struggles)
Easy, I won't hurt you. I promise.
*(sighs at the butterfly's
effort to get out)*
You're mad, aren't you?
I guess I'd be mad if I was locked up.

Disappointed, Kelly opens the lid.
Watching the butterfly fly away….

KELLY

Bye-bye.
(pause)
Sorry.

Kelly continues to watch it until it's out of
sight, then walks away with the empty jar.

"Birthday TMI"

BAILEY

You know what we're doing today?
First we're going to the park, then
we're going to the movies, then we're
going to have pizza at Chuck E.
Cheese. And cake and ice cream.

You know why?

Because on this day, 7 years ago, at
about 8:30 in the morning, my mom
leaned back in her hospital bed
(she leans back)
and yelled

AAARRRGGHHHH!!!!!!

(sweet smile)
And there I was.
Today's my birthday.

"What's Going On?"

DANNY runs to the living room excited….

> DANNY
> Wow! Were you guys watching that
> in here?! Iron Man and Thor were
> fighting Thanos, and Thanos was
> winning so Captain America …
> *(he stops. They're all quiet.)*
> What? What's going on? Why are
> you all staring at me?
> *(He reads their faces)*
> Wait. Is this about the fire in the trash
> bin? Listen, I can explain that! We
> had this old-fashioned fire starter and
> we wanted to see if the sparks would
> burn these papers like on Survivor.
> But then the fire got really big and it
> wouldn't go out. So we closed the lid
> ---we thought it would suffocate
> 'cause they told us in school that fire
> needs air to breath. I didn't know it
> would melt the lid!
> *(he sees their surprised faces)*
> This is about the fire in the trash…
> isn't it?

Uh-oh. If he wasn't in trouble before, he is now.

Note from the Coach:

In the previous scene "What's Going On?" Danny had a complete change of expression and emotion: he began excited/happy, but quickly saw the stares and had to backpedal. Here's Danielle's version:

DANIELLE excitedly runs into the room.

DANIELLE

Mom, mom! Did you just see that commercial!?! They have these new leopard-print tights that would really go with my dance top and ….
(sees their faces)
What? What's going on? Why are you all looking at me?
Oh no! Is this about the cat? I couldn't help it! It just kept coming around… it was so cute … and I only fed it a couple of times. And it needed a place to sleep so I let it in the garage. I was being nice! I didn't know it would get sick and throw up in your new car. I tried to clean it up.
(pause)
Wait. This is about the cat, isn't it?

Danielle's mom motions her over. She hangs her head and walks (downstage).

17

"We Got A Dog"

McNALLY

We finally got a dog! Wait 'til you
see him. We went to the shelter
yesterday – there were SO many dogs,
it was so noisy – and the first cage we
saw had this poor little puppy sitting
on the cement looking at me. He had
such sad eyes, like this …
>   (imitates: paws up, eyes big)
… so, I bent down near him and said
"hi, little buddy" and **GROWWLL!**
>   (jumps back)
He jumped at the cage and snapped at
my face! Sorry, not for me.
So we looked a little more and then---
I saw him. The cutest little half Lab,
half Pointer. As soon as I saw him I
knew; and he knew too. He stood on
his back legs and licked my fingers,
and yipped at me like he was saying
>   *(puppy voice)*
*"C'mon, take me home. Let me be
your dog."*
So I did. I named him Rocky. He's
my dog.

"Rich Without Money"

RORY

I wish my dad was rich. Morgan has a rich dad, and he travels all over the world. He brings her presents too, from everywhere. Big ones. If we were rich…. then I could have a swimming pool like they do, and a big new car. Morgan even has a nanny that takes care of her, and someone who cooks her dinner.

At our house, my mom cooks and takes care of us. And my dad comes home every day after work and plays with us in the back yard and shows us how to build things.

Morgan comes over here a lot, and we all play. I think she really likes it at our house.

I don't know why. It's not half as big as hers.

"Baby Secret"

DARBY

Hey, you wanna know a secret? Well,
if I tell you it won't be a secret
anymore … but I'll tell you.
I'm gonna have a baby sister. Real
soon. My mom's belly is way out to
here already.
>   *(holds out hands)*

And she went to the doctor and got
this little picture and you can see the
baby in it. All scrunched up like this:
>   *(bends in fetal position)*

I think she'll straighten out when she
comes out.
And I get to be the big sister.* I'm
gonna be a good big sister, and teach
her everything she needs to know.
Like how to wash between her toes in
the bathtub, to stay away from the
fireplace, and how much milk to put
on her cereal. The important stuff.
I'm gonna be a good big sister.

* or brother

© Bo Kane

"Tree Streamers"

JUSTIN runs in to Michael's bedroom.

JUSTIN

Michael! Wait 'til you hear this---
first, promise not to tell Mom or Dad.
Promise? Ok, did I tell you that Mia
told on Jacob for having his phone out
in class? She did. Class was already
over and she went up to the teacher
and told on him; so the teacher finds
Jacob in the hallway, takes away his
phone AND gives him detention.

Well, tonight Jacob got me and a
couple of other guys and we each
brought a roll of toilet paper, and
guess where we went?! Mia's house.
She's got two trees in front and we
sent streamers up to the top of them.
Shoom! You can't even see the house
we TP'd it so well! It was epic!

Hey, remember, whatever you do,
don't tell mom because … what?
What?!
Oh…She's standing right behind me,
isn't she? *(sigh)* Oh boy.

"Save The Drama For The Stage"

Megan talks about last night's rehearsal....

MEGAN

Ok. So we're supposed to be on stage
at five, that's the only time we could
get, and Rikki doesn't want to ride
with Sarah. I don't know why. So
Sarah's mom goes ahead without her
and Rikki has to walk and she's late.
And when they get there they all get
into an argument and they want ME to
side with Rikki who's mad at Sarah
for something I don't even know
about.

And Sarah suddenly doesn't feel like
dancing and Rikki is tired and mad, so
I'm trying to explain that nobody
meant to hurt anybody's feelings and
the next thing you know it's 5:30!
The rehearsal is half over and we
haven't even danced yet!

I got so sick of all the arguing, I hit
the music really loud, and went up
there and started our routine. I
danced by myself for a while, then
finally everybody stopped
complaining and came up.

MEGAN (cont'd)

And at the end of it, we had like about
a fifteen-minute rehearsal.
When I got home I called my big
sister and told her what happened.

She told me two things:
"Stay out of it" and *"Save the drama
for the stage."*
And that's what I'm gonna do.   Save
the drama for the stage.
     (dance position)
I'm a dancer, not a therapist.

© Bo Kane

Notes from the Coach:

* *"Play Outside"* (pg 13) is simply done with energy; a rare one--you play right to camera.

* In *"Butter-Fly"* (pg. 14), really see the butterfly (what color is it?), see it struggle, see it fly away. Take your time.

* In *"Birthday-Too Much Information"* (pg 15) Bailey's yell has to be real, as if you're in pain or lifting something heavy. A real (not phony-baloney) YELL, followed by a nice sweet smile. Also, say your own age.

* In *"We Got A Dog!"* (pg. 18), help us see the dog with your impersonations. Let that growl startle us; then show the pride.

* In *"Rich Without Money"*, (pg. 19) why do you suppose Morgan likes hanging out at Rory's house?

* In *"Baby Secret"* (pg. 20) Darby shows (not just tells) the baby's size and position.

* Our *"Tree Streamers"* prankster (pg. 21) shows us the tossing of the toilet paper with great pride. Let's see that enthusiasm, followed ultimately by the "uh-oh".

* In *"Payback"* (pg 26), Zoe takes the time to listen to Sabrina and her brother, and reacts to him telling her to, for example, "go see a movie" -- and hear him go crazy when she tells him she just sent another girl over to see him and his new girlfriend. Have fun being devious.

"Snake"

CHARLIE, a boy with a lot on his mind, approaches his dad with a request.

> CHARLIE
>
> Dad? Can I get a snake? For a pet. It doesn't have to be a big one. Maybe just a little one; but still a scary-looking one. Like a corn snake or something.
>> *(looks at Dad's questioning eyes)*
>
> See, some of the kids at school are mean to me … they don't think I'm tough. Because I'm not.
> But if I had a snake, they'd at least think I'm kind of cool. And I only have to take it to school and hold it in my hand one time. That's all.
> I'll take care of it, I promise.
> Can I get one?

He looks up at Dad with hope. He really needs to up his cool.

"Payback"

Pretentious Zoe is on her cell at the mall.

ZOE

You wouldn't believe what I found,
Sabrina! The cutest lip gloss in Triple
Shine Pink! *(listens)* I'm at the mall.
You are too?! LOL! I'll find you!
(her phone buzzes, she looks)
Hold on. It's my brother.
(clicks phone)
Hey Philip... *(listens)* No! I can't
hang out here a few more hours until
your 'girlfriend' leaves. I have dance
class at six. You said you'd pick me
up. You promised. *(listens)* No, I
can't just go to the movies. You stole
half my money!
(listens, then mischievous grin)
Hey, Philip, you know who I just ran
into? Lauren! Your old girlfriend
was right here at the mall. I told her
you were home and that she should
drop by and see you. Won't that be
nice?
(listens to "You WHAT?!")
Oh, that's right, you're with Amber.
My bad. Well, the three of you ...
have a good time.
(clicks him off, Sabrina on)
That'll teach him to keep his word.

ZOE (cont'd)
Sabrina? Meet you at the food court.

A sly grin as she walks to the food court.
Then, remembering ….
ZOE
Hey, 'Brina? Do you have any
money?

She walks off.

"An ounce of behavior is worth a pound of words."

- Sanford Meisner

"Mr. Pickles"

SOPHIA is sitting at a picnic table with two dolls, Mr. Pickles and Oscar, and some crackers and cheese.

SOPHIA
Mr. Pickles is hungry today, aren't you?   Would you like some crackers and cheese?
>(*Mr. Pickles voice*)

Why yes, I would like some crackers and cheese.
>(*Oscar voice*)

Hey, what about me? I like crackers and cheese too!
>*(Sophia glares at them)*

Aren't you both forgetting something?
>(*Mr. Pickles or Oscar voice*)

May we <u>please</u> have some?
>(*Sophia voice*)

That's better.   Here you go.   We have manners in our house. ….
All done? Ok, I'll eat the rest.
>(*sits back, eats, smiles*)

I always get the leftovers.

"Preventive Medicine"

ALEX, who has been invited to a class-mate's birthday party, sits in a chair with a worried expression.   Finally gathers the courage to talk to Mom about the problem.

ALEX

Mom?   Could you tell Tori's mom that I'm going to be sick tomorrow? That I have chickenpox or the measles, or one of those dangerous earaches or something? I just ... I don't want to go to that party.

Those kids play so rough, they laugh when you get hurt, and they spit their food all over when they talk and ...I don't really like them that much.
(gets an idea)
Hey! I know!   Tell them I have the flu, and with the money we save---on the present that we *don't* have to buy---we can go to the movies!

"Back In Time"

The year is 1900. A small bedroom with rickety furniture, and a young girl banished to it. She pulls a doll out of her dresser.

SADIE

Well, Raggedy, it's just you and me agin. Gonna be here all night, no dinner. I ain't hungry anyway, I had some bread on the way home from the schoolhouse. And all that hollerin' and puttin' me in here don't upset me this time. This time I got conviction.

I know Pa thinks he's doin' what's right. But it ain't. There was a whole war fought over that, and that war is done but he's still fightin' it. Prob'ly be fightin' it 'til he's dead.

That don't make it right neither. Either. Don't make it right 'either'. Miss Gwen would make me go to the board and do that sentence over again, wouldn't she?

Miss Gwen had us read the Declaration of Independence, and right there in ink it said that all men are created equal. Over a hundred years ago.

SADIE (cont'd)

They might have been created that way, but they sure don't get treated that way.   So I get sent to my room without supper for sayin' hello to a colored boy. I don't care.

I got everything I need right here anyway.   I got a window so I can look out and dream, and I got someone to talk to. Don't need nuthin' else. Anything else. Sorry Miss Gwen. I know you're helpin' educate me. In a whole lot of things.

"One Less Gamebuddy"

JAKE is in his room talking about his friend; (animated at first, then serious).

JAKE

My friend Wyatt lived just at the end of our block, and we used to do everything together. Walked to school, went to movies, had sleepovers when we were little.

A few days ago I was playing my Gamebuddy, and I was doing better than I ever had. Wyatt knocked on the door and asked me to come over to his house, but I told him I couldn't 'cause this was my best game EVER. He told me it was important, and I told him "not as important as <u>finally</u> getting to Level 10!"

He left, and I didn't see him for a few days. Then today I looked down the block and saw a big moving van in front of their house. I ran down there and the movers were just finishing. They said Wyatt moved out this morning. That's what he wanted to tell me. He wanted to say good-bye.

But I was too busy playing my game.

"Story Problems Are Easy"

RILEY sits in the kitchen doing homework.
Closing one book and opening another...

> RILEY
> That's it for spelling, now Math.
> Story problems.   These are easy.
> "If you're in a car going 20 miles per
> hour and you drive for 15 minutes,
> how far did you go? 20 miles an
> hour!?! What, is my **grandmother**
> driving?! Six blocks.
> *(he writes, then reads)*
> If 12 make a dozen, what is a gross?
> Mr. Kozinski's nose hairs. That's the
> Very <u>definition</u> of gross.
> Next. If plums are 75 cents a pound,
> and you need 5 pounds, how much
> would you have to pay? HAVE to
> pay?!? Nobody's making me pay
> anything for plums, I hate plums.
> *(he writes)*
> Zero. This stuff is so dumb.

Riley closes the book and walks away.

"Tough Teacher"

DANA marches out of school, angry with her teacher.

DANA

When I grow up I'm going to be a teacher, but I'm gonna be *nice* to kids. I'm not gonna punish <u>everybody</u> just because one kid gets us in trouble ....
(glares at a boy)
Carter.

Mrs. Johnson does that all the time, and it's not fair. WE didn't do it, HE did! So when I'm a teacher, everyone who was good will get to go home; I'll be fair and just punish that <u>one</u> kid.
(gets more animated)
And I'll punish him alright. I'll make him stay after school by himself, and write a thousand times on the board, and I'll make him stand in the corner, and I'll ....
(pause; she realizes what she's doing)
I'll be just like Mrs. Johnson.
(sighs)
Maybe I should just be a doctor.

"'I' Phone"

ARI is stretching on the floor of the gym.

> ARI
> So. We'd just finished our individual
> routines and were on a break. We
> went to this little area behind the
> trampoline…that's where they let us
> drink our smoothies; mine was from
> the machine, okay not great.
> Overpriced.
> Anyway, everybody pulls out their
> phones; I did too…my brother sent
> me a really stupid TikTok but it was
> funny. I put mine away 'cuz I wanted
> to talk about gymnastics but every-
> body was still on their phone so okay,
> I drank my smoothie.
> Then I said I thought we had a really
> good chance against Highland; that
> our floor routines were really good.
> Nobody looked up. I was talking but
> they were all like this:
> > *(mimics)*
> Instagrams and selfies. Lot of selfies.
> That was 20 minutes ago. I wonder if
> they noticed that I left.

"Pop Quiz"

JESSE walks toward his class and hears kids from the previous class talking about a quiz.

JESSE

A what? A quiz!? Oh no, today?
I'm not ready for a … wait, it has to
be on the Revolutionary War, right?
That's what we've been studying.
Washington, taxation without
representation, Declaration of
Independence. I got it. I know this
stuff. I think. What if it's about the
other one, the Civil War? No, she
wouldn't.
> *(grabs his phone, checks the time)*

One minute. Ok…. what do I
remember? …. Lincoln. Grant.
Slavery. Gettysburg Address, 1860's.
The Battle of the Monitor and the
Merrimack …. Hey! I know this
stuff, too. I'm there! A-plus coming
up. Bring on this test; Jesse Harrison
… is in the house!

He strides into the classroom.

Notes from the Coach:

* In "*Snake*" (25) Charlie has hope, then admits his 'cool' problem, then hope again. Don't be flat.

* In "*Mr. Pickles*" (28) Sophia gives each of her dolls a distinct voice. Maybe one high and one low. It might help to put her hand behind the doll and move it as it talks. (Harder than it looks, right?)

* "*Back In Time*" (30) is set over a hundred years ago, and Sadie is a Southern farm girl with an accent. And some real determination.

* "*'I'-Phone*" (35) is set in a gymnastics practice. Stretch, use your body, show us the selfies.

* "*Pop Quiz*" (pg. 36): Never heard of the Monitor and Merrimack? Hit up google, Sparky; it's part of knowing your character. He/She goes from worried to confident. A+ coming up... Use your own expression if you like.

* In "*Bad Words*" (page 38), Lee gets in trouble twice – both the mom, and then the dad, are mad at him. Play that line "*now we're both grounded*" realizing that his excuse got his dad in trouble too. His frustration can be funny to us, not to the actor playing him. (At the beginning, imagine someone saying '*c'mon, let's go!*)

"Don't play the result. If you have a character who's going to end up in a certain place, don't play that until you get there. Play each scene and each beat as it comes. That's what you do in life."
                                                                        - Michael J. Fox

"Bad Words"

LEE wears a sad look, answering a friend
who is waiting for Lee to go to "Fun Zone".

LEE
I can't go. I got in trouble today. For
saying a bad word. It just slipped out!
My dad says it every time somebody
cuts him off in traffic, but **I** get
grounded for it.
And now my mom says I can't go to
Fun Zone.
So I said *"if I can't go to Fun Zone
for saying bad words, why does Dad
get to go play golf on Sunday?! He
says 'em all the time!"*
(slumps)
Now we're <u>both</u> grounded.
And all I said was ….
*(about to say the bad word,
looks around, thinks better of
it)*
I better not. I'm in enough trouble.

"Science Camp"

ROBIN runs in through the door with a back-pack and a smile.

ROBIN
You wouldn't believe what I got to do at Science Camp this week! I got to shoot off a rocket, and we had lab coats and goggles, and …. me and my science partner made a real robot! It was so cool! We made him out of wire and steel, and we hooked up the batteries and it worked!
And Si
Then we raced all of the robots and ours won! First place! It was awesome.
You know what else we made? Slime! Real slime from real chemicals! Great slime fight.

Hey, did you know that Sirius is the brightest star? We saw all the constellations. Maybe I'll ask for a telescope for my birthday.
I think I'm going to be a scientist when I grow up.

"Homework Ogre"

Shane is at the teacher's desk coming up
with a 'reason' for his missing homework.

SHANE

I did the homework, really, but …
when I came out of my room with the
papers in my hand, uh …suddenly I
could feel this big wind swirling in
front of me. I took one more step, and
I was sucked right into the vortex and
the next thing I knew, I was falling
into a pit about a mile long!

When I landed, there was this fire-
breathing ogre who let out a fireball
and burnt everything around me.
I ran to get away, and when I was
going toward this castle I found this
sword stuck in a stone. I pulled it out
and flung it at him and when it hit him
he morphed into a giant bird, like in
Avatar, and he swooped me up and
carried me back into the vortex.

It took all night to make the journey
back, and when I got here… my
homework papers were gone!
But I really did the assignment. I
guess it just got burnt by the fire.
(lame or 'proud of the story' smile)

"Tooth Fairy"

Cassidy is pointing to a tooth in her mouth.

CASSIDY

I have a tooth coming out. It's this
one, right down here.
(shows the tooth)
I can wiggle it with my tongue. I'm
supposed to wait until it comes out by
itself, but I'm helping it a little bit.
Because when the tooth comes out
and you put it under your pillow, the
Tooth Fairy comes. And you get
money.
She buys up all the kid's teeth, then
takes them to a volcano and melts
them. And then she makes piano keys
out of them.

That's why when you see people
playing the piano, they're usually
smiling ---- the real teeth are smiling
at their cousins, the teeth in the piano.
It's true. My uncle told me.

"GOOAAALLL!"

ELIAS has a troubled expression and a basketball. He loves his dad, and doesn't want to disappoint him, but he'd rather play soccer than basketball.

ELIAS

My dad wants me to try out for the basketball team. He was a great basketball player; he once scored 40 points in a game. But ... I ...

(his expression says "I don't really like it." Then, he brightens up...)

I like soccer. Running down the sideline in the World Cup, get the pass and *(he kicks)* BOOM!

(He throws his arms up in the air like he just scored a goal).

Goooooaaalll!

(He takes in the crowd cheering for him, then... back to reality).

But my dad wants me to try out for basketball. So, I'm gonna try.
Wish me luck.

He grabs his basketball, tries to spin it on his finger --- no luck --- and heads for the door.

Notes From The Coach:

* In *"Homework Ogre"* (pg 40) Shane is trying to convince the teacher ... so describe it **vividly**. If you see the bird, the castle, the vortex (whirling air/tornado) we'll see it too. At the end he can either be sheepish in front of the teacher, or proud of his made-up story.

* In *"Tooth Fairy"* (pg 41) in the middle of Cassidy's story, she makes a confession that she's "helping it a little bit". This would be a good place to try a **stage-whisper**.

* Elias (page 42) is very animated in the middle of *"Gooaaallll!!!"* --- be physical, kick your leg, and love that game. Maybe don't overplay the dread of the basketball game; you're just trying to please your father.

* In *"Girl Trouble"* (pg 45) does Jack really like Sarah? Make a choice.

* In *"Two-Dollar Fortune"* (pg 46) Blake can show us his environment: does he or she have to whisper so Mom won't hear? Do we think the Clerk is smiling, or thinking *"No way, kid."*? Also, you can have an off-stage 'clerk' and improvise the ending; what can Blake get? Maybe a sample fragrance, a small necklace? Be creative.

* Have fun with *"All Things Animals"* (pg 47). Enjoy your 'hot dog' joke. Use your own name if you like.

"Target Practice"

JAMIE sees Mom looking at herself in the mirror, combing her hair over and over. This is the perfect time ….

                    JAMIE
Mom. Hate to tell ya, but …your hair isn't looking so good. And I think I know the problem. Split ends. But you know what? They have a shampoo for that. At Target. Come on, let's go!
We'll take care of that little problem of yours right now.
          (grabs mom's keys)
And as long as we're gonna be at Target, we might as well glance at those new super-phones that show movies in 3-D *and* have a million gigabytes! We should look at them while we're there. No sense making two trips. Let's go! I've got your keys.

Jamie walks away from the bathroom smiling like he (or she) has just pulled off the greatest trick in the world.

"Girl Trouble"

Jack is trying to explain how he got into trouble at school.

JACK

You know Sarah, right? Well, Sarah is always messing with me in class, especially when our teacher isn't looking. I think she likes me. But today she took my mechanical pencil and wanted me to get it back from her, 'cause … I think she likes me.

So I chased her – just to get my pencil back – and when she went around the table she fell. When our teacher turned around it must've looked like I pushed her, but I didn't! And I didn't want to tell on Sarah about the pencil … I don't know why I didn't … and I didn't want the whole class to get blamed, so, … I got in trouble.
      (*pause*)
Now I <u>know</u> she likes me.

"Two Dollar Fortune"

BLAKE walks up to the counter at a department store, looks over his/her shoulder to make sure Mom is not watching, then asks the clerk ….

> BLAKE
> "Excuse me; I have to buy something for my Mom. It's her birthday tomorrow. Can you help me? She likes soft things, like pillows, and scarves, and ... she's right over there…
> *(points, maybe whispers)*
> … she likes boots, and she's really pretty so she likes to smell nice. And red. She likes stuff that's red.
> *(reaches into pocket and pulls out three bills)*
> I only have three dollars. Do you have anything I can get for her? I'm kind of in a hurry."

He/she looks at the clerk and offers the crumpled bills, really hoping, trusting, that she can help out.

"All Things Animals"

A young News Reporter stands outside an animal shelter with a microphone.

REPORTER

Hi, this is Jo Baxter reporting for the "ALL THINGS ANIMALS" network. It's going to be a hot summer, so here are a couple of tips for your pets:

1)   Make sure your dogs and cats have plenty of water available all day long.

and

2)   NEVER leave your pet in the car in the parking lot, even if you crack the window.
The only "hot" dog that you want this summer …comes on a bun with relish and mustard!

This is Jo Baxter reporting for "ALL THINGS ANIMALS".
Now back to you in the studio.

"You Should Have Seen It"

JUSTIN runs in and tells his dad about his great game. His dad barely looks up from his iPhone…

JUSTIN

You should've seen our game today!
I was coming down the right side,
Brandon kicked the ball on kind of a
curve, like Messi kicks it, and I ran
right up to the ball, beat the defender
and WHAM!
Slammed it right into the goal.
(makes a kick motion)
It was great!   Greatest day I've ever
had. The whole team jumped on me!
It was the only goal of the game!   I
wish you could've been there, Dad.

His dad nods, doesn't look up.   Justin sighs.

JUSTIN (cont'd)
You might have been proud.

Justin turns and walks away.

Notes From The Coach:

* In *"You Should Have Seen It"* (page 48) Justin doesn't know, until the very end, that his dad doesn't care.   So he describes it with all of his enthusiasm and energy ... until the end. As you play Justin, see the top of dad's head, maybe even see him raise his index finger, as if to say *"One minute"*. But he never looks up. Justin still thinks he has a chance to make his Dad proud of him ... until the very end. Then, his shoulders slump, his eyes turn sad ... his whole body reacts.

* In *"Last Group Chat"* (pg. 50) really see and talk to your friends in that computer. Feel the pain and the uncertainty. And also the fact that *it's good to have friends to talk to.*

* For *"If I Only Had A Brain"* (51) you can use that song or sing your own song. But put yourself in dad's shoes; feel both his loss and his joy.

"Last Group Chat For A While"

Parker is at the computer. He/she is in pain, and in a video group-chat.

PARKER

Hey guys. I gotta go in a little bit, so … wish me luck. Some of you have been there, I know. Haley had her tonsils out; Charlie broke his arm. This is kind of like that, but kind of different too. They're going to cut right into my belly -- right here.
(points to his appendix)
Then they open me up, take out the appendix, and sew me back together again. It really hurts now, but if I let it go, it might break. Burst, I mean, and then there's all kinds of trouble.

So I won't see you all for a while. Maybe I'll be able to use my tablet in a couple of days.
Good thing my dad says it's okay to be scared. 'Cause I am. So … wish me luck. Wait, I already said that. Um, thanks everybody; really. Thanks. See you all later.

Parker closes the computer, looks at the door, grabs a backpack and bravely exits.

"If I Only Had A Brain"

SOPHIE

When I was little, at bedtime my dad would come in to my bedroom and he'd sing. Sometimes it was a goofy song, or one we heard in the car, or a Beatles song --- he loves the Beatles.

But most of the time, it was the scarecrow's song "If I Only Had A Brain" from The Wizard of Oz. We did it enough that he would leave out words and let me sing them. Like he'd sing (his voice) *I would not be just a nuthin', my head all full of* _____. And I'd sing "s*tuffin'*!"

But one day when he started to sing I told him I was too old for that now, and he could just say 'goodnight' to me. He took a second, then said "Ok. Good night." And every night since, he'd just smile and whisper 'goodnight' and leave.

And after a while, I missed it. I liked seeing him have fun singing to me. He once told me it was his favorite minute of the day.

She pauses, regrets taking that minute away.

SOPHIE (cont'd)

So last night I asked if we could sing
again. And that little smile of his got
big. I picked the scarecrow's song
and we sang the whole thing together.
*"...I could think of things I never
thought before. And then I'd sit ...
and think some more."*

I should never have told him I'm too
old for him.
If I only had a brain.

*This is the Scarecrow's song from the film
"The Wizard of Oz". You've seen the movie
(right?) and can Google the melody.*

Notes from the Coach:

* In "*Movin' Upstairs*" (pg. 54) you'll notice the year is 1959. Times were different and so was the style of speech. Kathy has a resolve; she does not for a moment feel sorry for herself. You can give her a light accent if you like, but certainly give the performance the real, raw truth. ('The Twilight Zone' was a very popular black-and-white tv show in the 50's and 60's).

* In "*Cat Wishes*" (pg. 55) you can physically get down by the cat in the middle of the monologue, then get back up at your "*indignation*". It makes it more fun to play.

* "*Canned Response*" (pg. 56) gives Sara the chance to show us her transformation in both expression and tone of voice. Let's see her go from "annoyed" and embarrassed to pleasantly surprised ... to happy.

"Movin' Upstairs, 1959"

1959, Midwest, USA. KATHY is packing up her clothing in the basement.

KATHY

I'm movin' upstairs now; gonna have a room like everybody else. My room. No more cold walls with daddy longlegs on 'em. I'm movin' to the bedroom that should have been mine in the first place. His "office." Hmf. Never did anything but drink beer and watch Twilight Zone in there. And now…he's gone. Finally. Never did treat my mama right. Complainin' all the time; slap her around if his meal wasn't exactly perfect. Last week after he yelled at her and stormed out I said, "Mama, I don't know why you stay married to him. He has never been nice to you not once in my whole life."
That hit mama hard; she just looked at me kind of stunned. Half-crying, half-determined. Two days later the cops and the judge told him "You've got to go." And now I'm moving upstairs. Mama and I painted it 'lavender'. It's not his office anymore. It's my room.

© Bo Kane

54

"Cat Wishes"

A not-too-happy ALEX comes in to the bedroom, drops her books, then looks at the cat lounging on her bed.

                    ALEX
Aren't you the lucky one? You don't
have math homework, and you
don't have boys sitting in front of you
making noises with their armpits, do
you? No, you just get to lie around all
day, maybe eat a little bit, then go out
in the yard and watch the butterflies.
Maybe climb a tree if you want. I
wish I were a cat.
          (gets near the cat)
And if I was the cat and you were me,
I'd roll over and let you scratch my
belly for a change.
And then you'd go get my food, and
I'd be the one who hears the can
opener and comes in meowing. How
would that be? But…. I guess you
can't tell me when you don't feel
good. And when you cough up
hairballs all over. So I guess …

No, wait --- you don't have to clean
it up, we do! It's like you have maid
service too. Yeah, I'd be a cat. What
a life.   © Bo Kane

                    55

"Canned Response"

SARA discovers the benefits of charity.

SARA

Ok, two things happened Monday.
First, I was leaving for school when
my mother asks where I put the bag of
cans. The what? Apparently, our
school has some kind of charity drive
and we're supposed to lug a bunch of
cans of peaches and soup and refried
doo-doo to give to a food bank. There
were like 20 cans in a Walmart bag.
Seriously, a Walmart bag.

Anyway, second thing … so, I go to
school trying to hide these stupid
cans; all I want to do is give 'em to
the lady and get out of that office.
And while I'm standing there, in
walks Wyatt -- quite possibly the
cutest boy in the universe but
certainly the best in our grade.

And what does he have in his hand?
A bag of canned food. He says, "*Hey,
Sara. You collect these too huh?
They really feed a lot of families.
Really cool of you to help.*" I didn't
even know he knew I was alive. Then
he smiled and said '*see you around.*'
Yes. Yes he will.   © Bo Kane

"Action Actor"

Michael gets inspired by a movie on tv...

MICHAEL
I was watching this tv show last night
and it had this kid in it who solved all
these crimes before the police did, and
he had the gangsters chasing him all
over the city. And I thought 'this is
so cool; I bet I could do that.'
So I told my dad 'I think I'd be a
pretty good actor'. He said *"what
kind of acting do you want to do?"*

I told him 'action-adventure'. Maybe
play a super-hero. He thought about
it, then asked me *"are you willing to
do the work?"* He told me the action-
adventure guys not only have to work
on their acting skills --- but they also
have to work out, and do stunts.
He said it was like pro football
players, or professional guitar players;
it takes a lot of work and 'focus'.

So I watched Avengers and
Mandalorian, and I thought "yeah, I
would put the work in. Seems like
you have to work hard no matter what
you do; why not do something cool?"

MICHAEL (cont'd)

[So ... I'll be in the play at school, take an acting class, and I'm already on the soccer team.] *

Yeah, I'm going to be an action actor. They'll still be doing those movies when I'm old enough to play one of those guys.

Michael ducks under an imaginary punch, then slings his "web" at the bad guy.

MICHAEL (cont'd)

This could be awesome.

Exit *(with style)*

*[optional]

"No matter what you're doing, do it with all the confidence of a 4-year old in a Batman t-shirt and cape."

- *Anonymous*

NOTES FROM THE COACH

*   In *"Action Actor"* (pg 57) Michael can give
his dad a thoughtful, studied voice that is
different from his own. Have fun at the
end, but play it real with the punches / web-
slinging.

*   In *"The Smokin' Truth"* (pg 63) there's no
need to whine. Just state the facts, then
come up with an 'almost the whole truth'
solution. Give yourself an accent if you
like.

*   In *"Tom Sawyer"* (pg 64) Chad has to hear
the aunt's part of the conversation—listen
and react. He doesn't get that his father
conned him into vacuuming, and won't until
after he reads the book. It's a fun scene;
take your time to hear her.

*   In *"Contagious"* (pg 65) it's different when
you hear an adult cuss and then, for the first
time, hear it from your friend. Funnier, yes.
But use the 'blankety-blank' (not the real
words) and have your smirking goofy fun.

*   *"Mom's Promotion"* (pg 67) deals with a
real dilemma and Kelly has that conflict in
her voice and in her face. Talk to your
(down-stage) brother; make him a real
brother.

"What Do You Think?"

MORGAN

We had an extra 10 minutes in class today, so our teacher told us to get some paper and write the answer to this question: *What do you think?* That's it. Usually it's 'what do you want to be when you grow up?' or 'what person would you like to meet and why?' but this was just 'What do you think?' I asked what he meant by that and he said "*What do you think?*" I should have seen that coming.

So I wrote that I think we should have less homework, and that all braces should be on the inside of our teeth. I think ghosts are real and rainbows are beautiful. I think that wars are stupid, and music is great. Singing a song should be our homework.

And I think I'd like to be a doctor, figuring out what's wrong with people and then helping them.

I think that would make me happy. Then the bell rang and we turned them in. And I thought about this assignment all the way home. Hmm. I think that's what it was all about.

"The Nap Report"

KADEN is forced to rest….

KADEN

I hate taking naps. But if I just yawn the next thing you know the shutters are closed and I'm in bed. On a Saturday!
I'm __ years old and mom treats me like I'm 4. My grandpa calls naps "mini vacations," but I don't. I call them jail.

The weird thing is---I have the strangest nap dreams. Not like at night. This one, I was back in kindergarten, but my cousins from Florida were there too, and my Aunt Jessica was the teacher.

She asked what we wanted to be when we grew up and I said "Superman". POOF! She took out this Harry Potter wand and I was flying through the air. And I saved this girl Sasha from a burning house. She's a girl from my 2nd grade class; I hadn't thought about her in years. And after I saved her from the fire, a spaceship landed.

KADEN (cont'd)

And just as the aliens were getting out --- I woke up.

Hmf.   Why was I thinking about Sasha? And what did the aliens look like? It's like the movie ended in the middle.
Next time I have to take a nap, I'll think of that spaceship landing and try to get back into that dream. Maybe, if I concentrate real hard, I can finish it. And then … I'll turn it in for a book report!

I'll get something out of these naps.

"The Smokin' Truth"

Mom is getting ready to go to her sister's
house. TAYLOR comes up with an excuse.

TAYLOR
Mom, can I **not** go to Aunt Sue and
Uncle Don's house? Could you say
I'm sick? No, wait, I don't want you
to lie. Lying is bad.
How about … that you forgot I had a
'party' to go to? I'll go over to
Tyler's or somebody's house and you
can just tell them I wasn't home.

It's not that I don't like them; I do,
but …it's just that they smoke all the
time. Their whole house smells like
smoke even when they're not
smoking. I hate that smell.

So if I call Tyler and tell her to invite
me over for a couple of hours, and
you tell Aunt Sue and Uncle Don that
I was at my friend's house for a
'party' --- don't worry, we'll have fun
so you could *technically* call it a party
--- then that's not lying. Is it?

She looks hopefully at mom, waits for the
reaction.

© Bo Kane

"Tom Sawyer Lesson"

CHAD is vacuuming when he feels his phone vibrate in his pocket. He shuts off the vacuum and answers it.

CHAD

Hello? Oh, hey Aunt Viv ... no, Mom doesn't get home until tomorrow. It's just me and dad here, and he's letting me use the vacuum! ... Yeah. At first he said no, that it's a complicated machine and I'm not ready yet. He was afraid I might bang in to the furniture or get something stuckin the motor, but I convinced him that I can handle it and be careful. ... Tom who? Tom Sawyer. No. ... it's a book? Ok, Mark Twain, got it. I'll look it up after I finish vacuuming. Well, I gotta fire this beast up again. When Mom gets home I'll tell her you called. Bye.
(pockets the phone)
Tom Sawyer can wait.
(looks at carpet)
Okay little fuzz-ball, YOU are history.

He fires it up and vacuums with a purpose.

"Contagious"

HARPER

My dad is a pretty good driver, but his brother ...whew. We were driving to Six Flags and my dad was in the front with him, and me and my cousin Mo were in the back. And things were fine, for about 5 minutes.

Out on the highway, a guy swerved in front of us and made Uncle Ted slam on his brakes. And I learned two more words I can't say out loud. That driver couldn't hear my uncle screaming at him, but we sure could.... *"You rotten blankey-blank, what the blank is wrong with you— you're gonna kill somebody!"*

So my cousin Mo pulled out headphones and handed me one. We plugged in to our phones and listened to music the rest of the way.

When we got to the park we rode four coasters and a two splash rides. One of the coasters was scary—I mean, <u>really</u> scary.

Mo got so scared she screamed *'holy blankety-blank, son of a blank!"*

HARPER (cont'd)
(wide eyes)
I couldn't believe it... neither could she. I just looked at her with big eyes and my mouth open.
She was cussing just like her dad! I yelled *"it's contagious!"* and we were laughing so hard we were crying--- upside down! Whew.

Not gonna lie, it was pretty funny.
Glad her mom wasn't there.
On the drive back home, we put the headphones on, and left them on.

"Try not to know something before your character knows it; play the moment your character is in right now. If he doesn't know that after he crosses the street his ice cream is going to fall off the cone and into the dog's mouth, then try to play him not knowing it until then. Let him be happy as he crosses the street."

© Bo Kane

"Mom's Promotion"

Late at night, KELLY looks at her brother.

KELLY

Scotty, you still awake? I can't sleep
either. (sigh) It's tomorrow. They're
coming **tomorrow**. I know we're
supposed to be thinking about Mom,
how happy she is to get this job.
Even Dad is quitting his job for her;
but I don't want to leave. I don't
want new teachers or new friends; I
want the friends I already have.
But the movers are coming tomorrow.
And Dad says *"no whining"* when
Mom is around. So this is it; last time
you'll hear me complaining. Mom
does so much for us, so … smiling
face for Mom. And, at least we have
each other, right? Right?

She looks at his contented sleeping face.

KELLY (cont'd)

G'night Scotty. You're right: just go
to sleep. Tomorrow's gonna happen,
whether I'm ready or not.
(leans on the pillow, rehearses)
*'No mom, it'll be great. We're all
proud of you. Really. It'll be fine.'*
(sigh)

NOTES FROM THE COACH:

*   There are a few layers for Carly to play in "*Jenna's Dilemma*" (pg 69). She is animated and big when she talks about Jenna's dad's truck and mom's feeling toward his girlfriend; but she is also small and sympathetic when she describes Jenna's exit in the truck (show us). And her solution, and her gratitude to her parents, is sincere.

*   In "*My Friend's Back!*" (page 71), apart from the obvious energy, there is a quick off-subject comment. Erin says, "*not complaining, everybody did*" apart from her enthusiastic sentence... in a different tone. Maybe a flatter tone. Almost like an 'aside' in theater, except that an aside is usually not heard by the other actor(s). Experiment.

*   "*Ring Pop*" (page 72) is just a fun bit where Jay really works dad over. You've done it yourself, haven't you?

*   In "*How's The Weather?*" (73) Adam didn't prepare, but makes a quick decision---and plays it to the hilt. As he sees his audience react he gets more ambitious ... taking it just a little too far. Be physical with the weather map, and don't worry if you get all of the lines exactly right. It's the performance that counts.

"Jenna's Dilemma"

CARLY unpacks her backpack and explains to Mom why her friend Jenna isn't with her.

CARLY

Jenna isn't coming to hang out here with me. She got a text saying that her dad was going to pick her up instead. They're having <u>his</u> weekend start early because, as you know, Jenna is coming with us on Sunday.

So Jenna's mom said he could have her today, instead of Sunday. That was their "arrangement".
Her mom and dad don't really like each other; they don't even pretend anymore. And her mom REALLY doesn't like the lady that lives with Jenna's dad.
> *(puts her claws up and snarls like a cat)*

Her dad is that exterminator, you know? He drives a big truck that says "KILLS BUGS DEAD!", and has that 3-D man hitting a cockroach on the head with a hammer on top of it.

I think it's funny; Jenna hates it.
> *(more)*

69

CARLY (cont'd)
So after school she got into the bug
truck, and when they drove away she
looked out the window like this ...
(sad face, small wave)
I'm glad you and dad are still
together. Really glad.

Hey, when Jenna comes over on
Sunday, do you think we could do
something fun. Like go see a funny
movie? I think she could use a
comedy.

*The pages of a script that we are reading for
an audition are called 'sides'.*

© Bo Kane

"My Friend's Back!"

ERIN excitedly rushes in to the kitchen …

ERIN

You'll never guess who I saw at the
pool! Brody Johnson! She's back!
Remember? We were best friends in
kindergarten and first grade, then she
moved away, to somewhere in
Michigan.
I was walking over to the diving
board and there she was. We didn't
recognize each other at first, then it
was "Ahhhkkk!!! We got so excited.

She had tried to call but we got rid of
our landline -- not complaining,
everybody did -- and she hadn't
enrolled yet, and … oh, who cares?!
She's back! This is going to be the
best summer ever!
> *(Erin turns, then turns back,*
> *looks around)*
Whoa. I gotta get ready. She's
coming over in about 10 minutes.
Maybe you could …. you know...

Erin makes a hand motion to the mess,
indicating to her mother to 'clean up'.

"Ring Pop"

JAY shows his ring pop to his friend.

JAY

This week my mom is on night shift
at the hospital, so that meant Dad had
to go to the grocery store. Which
meant I had to go too. (*dad voice*)
"*If I'm going, you're going.*" Not a
big thrill for me. Once you leave the
cereal and cookie aisle, it's pretty
boring. What kind of vegetables do
you want?' Seriously? None.

I couldn't even get any real speed
going on the back of the shopping cart
because it was so crowded.
We finally got to the checkout and I
see this red-sour Ring Pop. I said
"Dad, will you get this ring pop for
me?" And he says '*Two dollars!?*
No, put it back.'

So **I** said, "Let me ask this
another way: if I promise NOT to tell
Mom that you lost $50 on a White
Sox bet with Uncle Chris … now will
you buy me this ring pop?"
He called it 'blackmail'. I don't know
what that means, but I guess I'm good
at it.

"How's The Weather?"

ADAM

For 'Career Day' I was, um, going to
write something down, but…instead
of writing it, I thought I'd SHOW you
my career choice.

(stands up, points to a 'map')
Thank you, Ken. Now let's look at
the weather map.
If you look up to the north of us, you
see these little lightning bolts, and that
means trouble...lightning, heavy rains,
…raining cats and dogs, leaving--
poodles. Heh-heh. And to the west of
us we see snow in the forecast. Those
lucky kids are going to get a 'snow
day' off from school. We're not
going to get any snow; we're going to
have sunshine all day. But let's not
let those kids out west have all the
fun… what do you say we join those
snow kids out west, and take the day
off ?! Who's with me?!!

Adam drinks in the cheers and the laughter,
then sees the glaring eyes of the teacher.

ADAM
Yes, ma'am. Sorry.

He sits back down, subtly proud of himself.

Shake On It"

Brooklyn is confessing. To her dog.

BROOKLYN

Stella, I did a bad thing today. I made
fun of a boy at school today. He
didn't know the answer to an easy
question and I laughed and said
"duh!" really mean-like. Then other
kids laughed.

I have to tell him I'm sorry and I need
to practice. So you be him, ok? *'I'm
sorry for being mean yesterday, and I
won't do it again. We all don't know
the answer sometime. I'm sorry.'*
Shake.
    (she shakes with the dog)
Thanks, Stella. You're a good friend.

"Math Blues"

This math doesn't make sense
They're jus' messing with my head.
I'll never use this stuff
I should have stayed in bed.

Didn't finish my homework
And my mom did me wrong.
Put me in the 'home office'
Without a game or a phone.

Can't wait 'til I grow up
and don't have school every day.
"But how did you do in Math?"
young rapper.
Ain't nobody gonna say.

[Note: this can be done with 2 or 3 kids,
two lines at a time, or can be done as a solo
piece.]

© Bo Kane

"When you hit a wrong note, it's the next note you hit that makes it good or bad."

-Miles Davis

The great trumpeter/musician Miles Davis is saying that if you make a mistake, mess up your line, that's not so bad. It's what you do after it that makes it good or bad. The real artist corrects it or makes up for it seamlessly and believably.

Acting Scenes

Scene [seen] - *noun*
a unit of action or a **segment of a
story** in a play, motion picture, or
television show.

"Smackdown"

A BROTHER is watching TV when his
SISTER enters.   He quickly changes the
channel on the remote.

> SISTER
> What are you watching?

> BROTHER
> Uh… this. Whatever it is.

> SISTER
> Real housewives?!   Yeah, right.
> What WERE you watching?
> > *(grabs the remote, hits 'back')*
> Fighting?!

> BROTHER
> It's Friday Night Smackdown!
> Cowboy Hulk versus The Master of
> Disaster!   Aaarrrghhh!

He punches the air, then flexes.

> SISTER
> Does Mom know you're watching
> this!?
> BROTHER
> No, don't! … Mom doesn't need to
> … wait...

She yells out as she leaves the room.

>   SISTER (cont'd)
> MO-OM!   Did you know Blake is
> watching people beat each other up on
> TV??!

>   BROTHER
>   *(to himself)*
> She does now.

He plops back down, hits the remote back to ... whatever.

"Skateboard Champ"

A REPORTER holds a microphone and interviews the new skateboard champ, CASEY FLASH.

> REPORTER
> *(to camera)*
> Hi I'm Dana Smith, reporting from the Long Beach Skate Park where Casey Flash has just won the half-pipe championship.
> *(to Casey)*
> Congratulations Casey.

> CASEY
> Thanks Dana. The rest of these skaters are really good, but I guess I got lucky today.

> REPORTER
> It was more than luck. You really put on a show out there. What do you think won it for you today?

> CASEY
> I think the judges liked the 3-60 that I pulled at the end. I got a lot of air, and had fun with the twist.
> So, yeah, I think it was my ending.

REPORTER
And that 3-60 ending got Casey
Flash a first-place trophy. Anything
you want to say to the skateboarders?

CASEY
Yeah. Have fun, catch some air, but
… (*points to his helmet*)
protect your brains. Wear a helmet.

REPORTER
Good advice, Casey.
(*wrap-up to camera*)
That's it from the Long Beach Skate
Park. I'm Dana Smith, now back to
you in the studio.

© Bo Kane

"Bugs"

CODY and KATIE are lying on the picnic table looking at bugs.

CODY
Hey look at this one.

KATIE
What is it?

CODY
I think it's a June bug.

KATIE
Aren't June bugs brown?   This is black.

CODY
Well, it's not a beetle and it's not a roly-poly. I know what those look like.

KATIE
Don't squish it! It might be a daddy bug going home to his wife and kids.

CODY
I'm not going to squish it.   I'm just looking at it. Off you go, little bug.

He puts it into the grass.

> KATIE
> He's probably going to go home and
> say "Whew! You wouldn't believe
> what happened to me today! I was
> almost squashed by a monster!"

> CODY
> *(bug voice)*
> "But I wasn't squashed, thanks to
> 'Bug Hero Man!'"

> KATIE
> *"And his super-powered friend,
> "Super Insect Girl!"* Wait, that
> doesn't sound so good. *"Bug Hero
> Woman! Protector of All Living
> Creatures, and ..."*

> CODY
> *(interrupts)*
> Ok, ok, Hero Woman; let's see if we
> can find some more.

> KATIE
> Here's a roly-poly. Don't be afraid
> little buggy, I won't hurt you.

They both gently touch the bug in her hand.

"I Before E"

MORGAN and ALEX are looking at their spelling homework.

> MORGAN
>
> Spelling doesn't make any sense!
> "Way" like "no way" is spelled right,
> but if I 'weigh' myself it's spelled
> w-e-i-g-h. Really?!

> ALEX
>
> It's weird, but it's right. *"I before E
> except after C, or when sounded like
> 'A' as in neighbor and weigh."*

Morgan glares at Alex.

> MORGAN
>
> You made up a rhyme for this?

> ALEX
>
> Somebody did. Weird, huh?

> MORGAN
>
> Ok, riddle me this, Batman. If the
> "gh" in weigh sounds like nothing,
> why does it sound like 'F' in
> 'enough'?

ALEX

I don't know. Why do they use a
"ph" to sound like an "F" in
telephone?

MORGAN

That's what I'm talking about! At
least in math, 2+4 always equals 6.
Not sometimes, all the time!   In
spelling, 'gh' can sound like F, 'ph'
can sound like an F, and hey!   Sometimes an F sound is spelled with
…an F!   Who invented this stuff?!

ALEX

Well, it's called "English" so …..

MORGAN

That figures. Anybody else would
spell "tea" t-e-e.

ALEX
(English accent)
"What say, my lord; why not throw an
'A' in there just to mix it up a bit?"

MORGAN

And what about tough, through and
though?   *(more)*

MORGAN (cont'd)
They're not only spelled with an
"o-u-g-h" which is ridiculous, but
they sound completely different!

ALEX
Ok, ok. You made your point. You
want to study math?

MORGAN
No.

ALEX
Ok then. Let's keep going. Spell
'knock'. Here's a hint: the first "k"
is silent but the second one isn't.

MORGAN
This is hopeless.

Morgan drops face-down in her book.

ALEX
Wait 'til we get to "imagination".
The "t-i" sounds like an "s-h".

Morgan lifts her face just to give Alex an
evil stare, then, drops it back down.

© Bo Kane

Notes from the Coach:

* In each scene it's very important to listen to your scene partner, hearing the dialogue as your character does: for the very first time.

* Your entire body is your instrument, not just your voice. Your voice will change with your emotions, and so will your facial expressions and body language. Try not to be stiff; most of the time we let our body match our emotion.

* Read the stage direction and the parentheticals. Not just the dialogue. You may choose to change some of it, but as least take into consideration what the writer intended.

* Even if you paint your character with big, broad strokes, be believable. Nickelodeon and Disney casts often play very big, sometimes cartoony characters, but because they stay **true** to their characters, we believe it.

* If you or your scene partner says the wrong cue or drops a line, it's no big deal. Stay in character and keep going. In real life, we don't always know what the other person is going to say.

"Football For Real"

AUSTIN and TREVOR are in the living room while their mothers go to the kitchen.

AUSTIN
So, what do you want to do?

TREVOR
Let's play something.

Trevor starts looking through his video box.

AUSTIN
Let's play football!

TREVOR
We can't. I broke that game.

AUSTIN
I mean outside. With a football.

TREVOR
Outside? Football for real?

AUSTIN
Yeah. I brought one. We can throw it around in the front yard.

TREVOR

I've never really thrown a football
for real.   But I can make Joe Burrow
throw it great on my game.

AUSTIN

Ok. You be him on the Bengals.   I'll
be Patrick Mahomes. Let's go.

He heads toward the front door. Trevor puts
down his video games, hesitates.

AUSTIN (cont'd)

And when we've worked up a
sweat, we'll come in and play
video games. Ok?

TREVOR

We're gonna sweat?!

AUSTIN

Yeah. Come on!

Austin tosses the ball to Trevor, who
bobbles it like a hot potato. He follows
Austin out the door with a sigh and a
worried expression.

© Bo Kane

"Tossin' Trash"

LUCY and PAIGE rehearse their PSA in front of Paige's *(off-camera)* big sister.

PAIGE
We have to do a media presentation, so we picked a Public Service Announcement.

LUCY
It's a PSA about cleaning up the beaches. See what you think.

PAIGE
Ahem...(to camera) Hi, I'm Paige.

LUCY
And I'm Lucy. We both like a lot of the same things: we both like movies.

PAIGE
Especially comedies.

LUCY
Romantic comedies for me. And we like hip hop music.

PAIGE
And cheeseburgers!

LUCY *(to Paige)*
Actually, I don't eat red meat.

PAIGE
Oh. Scratch the burger ad-lib.

LUCY *(to camera)*
And we both like summers at the
beach.

PAIGE
But there's one thing we don't like —
littering.

LUCY
Littering can turn a paradise … into a
dump.

Paige picks up a can and a candy wrapper.

PAIGE
So enjoy your food and drink, and
then find a trash can.

LUCY
Let's keep our parks and beaches
clean.

PAIGE (or BOTH)
'Cause tossin' trash ... ain't cool.

LUCY *(to off-screen sis)*
What do you think? I think we should
be on TV!

91

"Pants on Fire"

Two kids are sitting at the school computer. ELLIOTT grabs the mouse from SABRINA.

ELLIOTT
Ooh, I got an idea, give me that! Uh-oh.

It drops, shatters. He puts it into her hand.

ELLIOTT (cont'd)
Here, you take it!

SABRINA
Don't give it to me! What are we gonna do? She's gonna find out and know we broke it!

ELLIOTT
So, we tell her we didn't.

SABRINA
What?!

ELLIOTT
We tell her ... we were just coming from the restroom and we found it like that. She's been in the front of the room, she won't know. We'll tell her we weren't even here.

SABRINA
That's called 'lying'.

ELLIOTT
Yeah, and your point is …?
Look, just do it right and we won't
get in trouble.

SABRINA
I can't lie!

ELLIOTT
'Brina, we're not … lying. Exactly.
We're acting. You always wanted to
be an actress. Just let me do the
talking, and you *'act'* like I'm telling
the truth.

SABRINA
No. I'm going to go tell her it was an
accident, and that my dad will get the
school a new mouse and that we're
sorry. <u>That's</u> the truth.

She gets up and walks to the front of the
room. He watches her go.

ELLIOTT
She's gotta learn how to act.

"It's Gonna Explode!"

A science kit with jars of colored liquid sits in front of ARCHIE. KASEY picks up a jar of blue liquid.

> KASEY
> Ooh, a chemistry set. Do you know what you're doing?

Archie takes the jar from him and swirls it.

> ARCHIE
> Of course not. That's why it's called an experiment. Let's pour that chemical into this one, and then mix 'em together.

> KASEY
> Cool. We can be like mad scientists.

Archie does a low, evil laugh as he holds his jar still. Kasey pours in the other chemical. They set it on the table, and watch.

> KASEY (cont'd)
> Oooh, smokin'. These chemicals don't like each other.

Archie picks up another bottle.

ARCHIE
This says "never mix with
formaldehyde."

Mischief in their eyes...

KASEY
Let's do it!

They pour and watch the two liquids smoke.
Then bubble. They laugh.

ARCHIE
It looks like it's gonna explode.

KASEY
Yeah! Cool.

Then, their smiles turn to *UH-OH!"*
Their eyes get big … and …...!!!!

ARCHIE
I'm outta here!!

KASEY
Wait for me!!!

They run out.

© Bo Kane

"Stolen Keys"

Taylor is in the library; Callie RUNS IN.

> CALLIE
> Here! Hide these room keys!
> Whatever you do, don't tell Mrs.
> Baker where you got 'em cause
> I DIDN'T DO IT!

She drops them like a hot potato.

> TAYLOR
> Neither did I!...What didn't I do?!
> Why do you have her keys?

> CALLIE
> Some guys were playing a trick on her
> and locked her out of her room, and
> they just shoved them at me and ran!

> TAYLOR
> So you just hand them to me?!
> Thanks a lot.
>   (looks, thinks)
> Wait. I've got it. We'll just leave
> them at the librarian's desk, then
> pretend we're sick and go to the
> nurse's office. When she finds the
> keys, we'll be way over there.

CALLIE

Great idea.   You're the best friend I ever had.

They do a pinkie handshake.

TAYLOR

Friends forever.

They cough and sneeze their way toward the desk, but just as they are about to drop the keys and run…

MRS. BAKER (O.S.)

Girls! Are those my keys?!?

They freeze in their tracks, eyes big. Then--- they turn and POINT AT EACH OTHER.

BOTH

She did it!!

(Mrs. Baker is an off-screen or off-stage voice).

"Tattle-Tale"

An older BROTHER sneaks into the kitchen, sees the candy jar. He looks around, then slowly lifts the lid. As he reaches in he is STARTLED by …

> LITTLE SISTER
> Busted!!

> BROTHER
> Ahhh!!

The lid drops; he tries to catch it and fumbles it, making even more noise.

> LITTLE SISTER
> You're in trouble now.

> BROTHER
> You little … you better not tell Mom.

> LITTLE SISTER
> What'll you give me if I don't?

> BROTHER
> You mean, what'll I <u>do</u> to you if you do.

> LITTLE SISTER
> Then you'll be in even more trouble.

He knows she's right.

BROTHER
Ok, I didn't mean that. I'll be nice
to you for a week, just be quiet.

LITTLE SISTER
Two weeks.   And a dollar.

BROTHER
A dollar! It's only a piece of candy.
(pause)
You know what? Go ahead and tattle.
Do it. Just remember: <u>Nobody</u> likes
a tattle-tale. Not even Mom.

LITTLE SISTER
Ok! One week. And a quarter!

BROTHER
(over his shoulder)
Tattle-tale brat.

He's gone.

LITTLE SISTER
(to herself)
I've got to work on my negotiation
skills.

99

Notes from the Coach:

* Our *"Skateboard Champ"* (page 80) can wave to the crowd, and be a humble (or not-humble Champ). Best to hold the mic near the Champ, and tilt it back and forth.

* In *"Bugs"* (page 82) you can use 'prop' bugs, or your imagination.

* *"I Before E"* (pg. 84) is a fairly long scene (but seriously, haven't you wondered about this spelling stuff before?). Anyway, if you need to, cut it down. Maybe cut from "Who invented this stuff?" all the way to "Ok, ok, just spell 'knock'. Ps... did you get the joke behind *"weird, huh?"* "Weird" doesn't follow any of those rules!

* In *"Tossin Trash"* (pg 90) the PSA part is played right to camera. Lots of interaction, and a 'reaction' to the meatless revelation.

* In *"Pants On Fire"* (pg 92) Elliott sees nothing wrong with lying to get out of trouble. In his mind, it's perfectly ok.

* In *"It's Gonna Explode!"* (pg. 94) you can just use 2 glasses, a little bit of water .... and a little bit of imagination.

* In *"Stolen Keys"* (pg 96) remember that they are in a library, so adjust your speaking voices. Using props, like keys (dropping them like they're hot) can be fun; same with the quick change from 'best friends' to 'she did it!' Be expressive.

* In *"Tattle-Tale"* (pg. 98) both Brother and Sister have a change of strategy in mid-scene, so the actors will change their voice and body posture too.

* In *"I'll Cover For You"* (pg 102) Aidan begins near tears but he grows up in this scene, and is willing to take his punishment.

* In *"Bully Girl"* (pg 104) we'll need to see some real affection from the brother and sister at the end of the scene, as he thumps her (gently).

* Will has to make a quick facial expression change in the middle of *"The Eyes Have It"* (pg 106). He **almost** teases his friend, but decides to **be** a good friend instead. At first, have fun making your own sound effects.

* For *"Let It Go Already"* (pg 108) Carlin is making lyrics up in the moment; he's good at it, but he shouldn't make them up too fast.

* In *"Sleepover"* (pg 118) Caitlin could be a nice girl who's offended by the lack of trust, or a not-so-nice girl who wants Sabrina to fall asleep and play another trick on her.

* In *"Unnecessary Roughness"* (pg 120) Coby starts out sad/frustrated, but ends up with a ray of hope. Jake needs him (Coby is the only decent quarterback) so he's going to try anything---even talking to Coby's mom.   Play him with some energy.

"I'll Cover For You"

AIDAN is cowering in the closet when his older sister MARLEY approaches.

MARLEY
Are you hiding from Mom?
(he nods 'yes')
How come?

AIDAN
I broke her favorite clock.

MARLEY
On purpose?

AIDAN
No! I was just swinging my light saber and I didn't see it.

MARLEY
Just tell her it was an accident.

AIDAN
But she's gonna be mad! She loved that clock. Grandma gave it to her.

MARLEY
Well you shouldn't have been swinging a light saber in the living room.

AIDAN
I'm sorry!

He begins to break down. Marley feels for him, puts her hand out to help him up.

MARLEY
I know. Listen, I'll tell her I did it. I haven't been in trouble in a long time. Come on.

He takes her hand and gets up. They turn, and look up to see MOM.

MARLEY
(to Mom)
Mom, I'm sorry, I didn't mean to…

AIDAN
(interrupting)
Mom, I broke the clock and I'm really sorry. I promise to never do it again.
(whispers to Marley)
Thanks anyway.

Marley puts her arm on his shoulder. He's growing up.

"Bully Girl"

A SMALLER GIRL walks up to a table with a lunch bag. Just as she pulls out a chair, a BIGGER GIRL grabs the chair and pulls it away like a bully.

>   SMALLER GIRL
> Hey! I was going to sit there.

>   BIGGER GIRL
> Well, now you're not.

>   SMALLER GIRL
> That's not fair. You can't do that.

>   BIGGER GIRL
>   *(in her face)*
> What are you going to do about it?

Unseen by the Bigger Girl, the Smaller Girl's big BROTHER walks up behind the Bigger Girl.

>   SMALLER GIRL
> I'll tell my brother.   Or maybe I don't have to.

>   BIGGER GIRL
> And why not, Wimp?

SMALLER GIRL
'Cause he's standing right behind you.

The Bigger Girl turns to see the BROTHER glaring at her.

BROTHER
Don't ever threaten my sister. Got it?

The Bully looks up at him, then turns and runs out. The Smaller Girl sits down.

SMALLER GIRL
Thanks.

BROTHER
No problem. Hey, she doesn't have a big brother, does she?

SMALLER GIRL
She's got a brother, but he's only 4.

BROTHER
I can probably handle him.

SMALLER GIRL
Yeah. …. Probably. *(giggles)*

He thumps the back of her head as he exits.

105

"The Eyes Have It"

WILL and CLINTON are shooting squirt-guns at a target at the County Fair. Will is hitting well; Clinton is getting frustrated.

BOTH

Pow! Pow! Swoosh! Bam! Awww.
Gotcha! C'mon! Awww.

They stop, out of time and quarters. Will gets a prize thrown to him.

WILL

Alright! That's the best I've ever done!

CLINTON

I hardly hit any. I think this gun is off.

WILL

I used that squirter last time, and I won a prize then, too.

CLINTON

Yeah. And I didn't hit with that other gun either.

WILL

Maybe you need glasses.

CLINTON

Glasses!? I don't want to look like a nerd!

Will is about to be a wise-guy, and say something like *"too late, you already look like a nerd*!" But he stops himself from saying it when he sees how upset Clinton is.

WILL

Uh…you won't look like a nerd. You'll look smart. That's all.

CLINTON

You think?

WILL

Sure. Real smart. Smart is cool. C'mon. Let's go to the Funhouse.

They walk away, Clinton considering glasses, Will wears a *"whew, I almost insulted my friend"* look on his face.

© Bo Kane

"Let It Go Already"

CARLIN is reading when MAKENA enters.

MAKENA
Hey, Carlin, are you going to be in the
Talent Show?

CARLIN
Uh …. no.

MAKENA
It'll be fun.   I'm going to be in it.

CARLIN
Good for you. You're not doing that
Taylor Swift routine again, are you?

MAKENA
No! Everybody does that. I'm going
old school cartoon--the song from
"Frozen".

CARLIN
Why did I even ask?

MAKENA
Hey, you're really good at…

CARLIN
No.

MAKENA
I haven't even asked you yet.

CARLIN
No.

Makena ignores the 'no' and gears up to
perform her changed version of *"Let It Go"*.

MAKENA
Here's the start: it's like Idina's
"Let It Go".....
"Don't let them know,
don't let them see,
That I'm as nervous as I could be
Conceal don't feel
Don't let them knooooow
They'll never knoooooooooow.
Let it go! Let it go!" ....

CARLIN
Hold it! Ok, I get it. It's all about the
audition for the talent show. Clever,
sort of. Why don't you add some
lyrics about school too? The teachers
will be right there.

MAKENA
Like what?

CARLIN

Like, uh …'grades never bothered me anyway.'

MAKENA

Great idea! I knew you could help.

CARLIN

Oh no. I could, but I'm not.

MAKENA

You can't or you won't.

CARLIN

I'm not.

MAKENA

I can't tell if you're chicken, or you just think you're too good. I'll go with chicken. *buck buck buck buck.*

Carlin sighs. He puts his book down.

CARLIN

Ok. Sing something about that you're too busy in the talent show to do homework, so you're just letting it go.

She motions to him to go on.

CARLIN

Like …..um (*talk-sing*)
'I don't care…what they assign today
Let me sing in the plaaaaay.
Grades never bothered me anyway.'

MAKENA

I knew you'd say 'yes'. We're in!!

She runs out, excited. Carlin protests …

CARLIN

I didn't say yes, I ….

… he's talking to thin air. Frustrated, he
picks up his book and walks out....

CARLIN (cont'd)
(to himself, to Frozen's tune)
"Tell her no, tell her no, why didn't
you just shut your mouth after 'no'?"

He hits himself in the head with the book.

Let It Go © 2013, written by Kristen Anderson-Lopez and
Robert Lopez.

"Español"

EMILY sits practicing her Spanish when
MICHAEL walks up.

EMILY
(to herself)
¿Que pasa?

MICHAEL
Nada. What are you doing?

EMILY
Trying to learn Spanish.

MICHAEL
Why?

EMILY
There's a woman who lives on my
street, and she doesn't speak English
very well. But she's really nice and
makes cookies, so I wanna talk to her.

MICHAEL
That's cool. But everybody knows
the word "hi". It's hola. You could
just say that. Or just smile at her.

EMILY
I do, but I wanna do more than that.
Do you want one of her cookies?

MICHAEL
Sí, gracias. Hey, these are bueno!

EMILY
That's right! Your mom speaks
Spanish. Say "these are good."

MICHAEL
Estos son deliciósos. Or just say
¡Que rico! One more?

EMILY
Ok. How do you say 'one more'?

MICHAEL
Uno màs. Do you want me to walk
over there with you?

EMILY
Would you? That'll be great! You
should taste her fajitas.

MICHAEL
Whoa, this just keeps getting better.

And off they go.

"Take It From Me, Kid"

Louie is starting his first day at school, and his big brother Isaac is giving a few tips.

ISAAC
Now that you're going to real school, you need to learn a few things about teachers and classrooms and stuff.

LOUIE
Like what?

ISAAC
Like, in kindergarten they let you just throw your backpack on the floor. Not anymore, buddy. You get a locker.

LOUIE
Really? Cool!

ISAAC
Yeah, and you don't go home at lunch time, either. You eat lunch here. And here's a tip: always use a straw. 'Cause if you tip your milk over your mouth some kid will bump you, trust me. And you'll be wearing your milk.

LOUIE
I can still take my Avengers to the
lunchroom, can't I?

ISAAC
Uh, sorry, Louie; no Avengers.
You're all grown up now.   Gotta
leave 'em at home.

LOUIE
I...I...can't?

Louie looks shocked, almost ready to cry.

ISAAC
Ok, you know what? Take 'em in
your backpack. And if your teacher
finds 'em, tell her your big brother
said it was ok.   I've still got a lot of
pull around here.

Louie shoves them into his pack, smiles a
'thanks'. Isaac puts his arm on his shoulder.

ISAAC (cont'd)
I think you're ready, kid. Let's go.

"Cousins"

Two kids ride the bus home from school.

MARSHALL
Hey, Zoe, what are you doing this
weekend?

ZOE
On Saturday I'm going over to my
cousins'. They live on a ranch and
they just got a new dog that's
gigantic!

MARSHALL
Wow, cool. I wish I had cousins.

ZOE
You don't have cousins? Everybody
has cousins. I even have cousins in
Europe.

MARSHALL
Not me. My mom is an only child
and my dad's brother hasn't gotten
married yet.

ZOE
That's too bad. Cousins are like your
friends, but they're your family too.
It's like a double friend.

MARSHALL
I know. I just don't have any.

Zoe thinks about it for a moment.

ZOE
Hey! I'll be your cousin. We'll tell
people that our moms are cousins.
That would make us like ... second
cousins or something.

MARSHALL
Yeah! Like cousins once replaced.

ZOE
Yeah.   And maybe you can come to
the ranch with me. You want to?

MARSHALL
Sure. I'll ask my mom.

The bus pulls to a stop, Zoe gets up.

ZOE
Me too.   See you later, cuz.

Marshall smiles. She has a cousin.

"Sleepover"

SABRINA and CAITLIN are in the school hallway…

CAITLIN
I've got to go and get my piano lesson finished so I can go to Amber's slumber party. It will be so cool. I'll see you there.

SABRINA
Uhh … I don't think so.

CAITLIN
What? You were invited.

SABRINA
Yeah, I was invited last time, too.

Sabrina gives her a *"remember?"* look.

CAITLIN
Oh, yeah, the water trick. Sorry. But you know that we were just having fun….and we know you have a great sense of humor.

SABRINA
Yeah, right.
(more)

SABRINA (cont'd)
Look, I have dance, homework, and
music lessons … and I go to bed
early. And I NEVER want to be the
first one to fall asleep at a slumber
party. Never again.

CAITLIN
You won't be! And even if you did,
we won't play any tricks on you. I
promise we won't.

SABRINA
Thanks, but … have fun.

CAITLIN
What? Don't you trust us?

They look at each other for a long moment.

SABRINA *(softly)*
No. It was really embarrassing, so …
no. See you Monday.

Sabrina walks away. Caitlin starts to call
after her *("okay, fine!")* but doesn't. She
stands alone in the hall, figuring out that you
can't just ask for trust. It has to be earned.

119

"Unnecessary Roughness"

JAKE catches up to COBY after school.

> JAKE
> Hey, Coby! Try-outs for flag football
> are tomorrow. Did you forget to sign
> up?

> COBY
> No.

> JAKE
> I didn't see your name on the list. Did
> you ask your mom?

> COBY
> Yeah.

> JAKE
> What did she say?

> COBY
> Did you see my name on the list?

> JAKE
> No.

> COBY
> That's what she said.

JAKE

C'mon, you gotta play football.
Who's gonna throw the ball to me?

COBY

Don't know.

JAKE

Why can't you play?

COBY

My mom says it's dangerous and she
doesn't want me to get hurt.

JAKE

Does she know that you don't tackle
in flag?   That hardly anybody ever
gets hurt?

COBY

I don't know.

JAKE

You didn't tell her that?! You gotta
tell her.   She probably thinks we
tackle.

COBY

Yeah, maybe.   I didn't think of that.

JAKE
Come on, we need you at quarterback.
I'll go home with you and we'll tell
her together.

COBY
You will?

JAKE
Yeah! I need somebody who can
throw passes to me. Let's go.

Coby follows him with a new hope and a
new sense of purpose.

© Bo Kane

Notes from the Coach:

* There are shocks that are bad (spill your
   milk all over your homework) and shocks
   that are good (reach into your pocket and
   find a lost 5-dollar bill). In *"Trading
   Lunches"* (pg 124) Jordan gets a bad shock
   (he just traded away his favorite lunch) and
   Darby gets a good shock. Don't let your
   expression give away what's in the lunches
   until you open them.
   And yes, "Lunch-munchie" can be hard to
   say; it's a good time to practice enunciation
   (speaking clearly).

* In *"I'll Say A Word..."* (pg 126) Lindsey
   likes being in control, but in the end learns a
   lesson, and the regret shows on her face.

* *"Poetry"* (pg 132) needs little explanation.
   I think it's funnier not to say the word in
   Andrew's 'poem' but to **almost** say it.
   Needs good timing on the interruptions.

* In *"The Tryout"* (pg 134) Jake goes from
   worried to hopeful ... with a little help from
   his friend. Let his gratitude show. And at
   the end, when he takes a few pretend swings
   before he leaves--go for it!

* For *"Life's Not Fair"* (136) Keegan resents
   his sister's rules, but instead of complaining,
   he shows her---by holding the books up high
   and letting them SLAM to the floor. Smirk.

"Trading Lunches"

School cafeteria. JORDAN looks at his
lunch box, looks over at DARBY's.

JORDAN

Wanna trade lunches?

DARBY

Maybe.   What have you got?

JORDAN

I don't know.   It's a surprise.

DARBY

Like a peanut butter and jelly
surprise?   I don't think so....

JORDAN

I'll throw in 50 cents.

DARBY

Hmmm....ok.

He takes Jordan's lunch (and his 50 cents),
opens it up and --- a really good shock.

DARBY (cont'd)

Whoa! Lunch-munchies! Alright!

JORDAN
What?!? My mom didn't tell me she
bought Lunch-munchies! She's never
bought those before.

DARBY
I love these!
(*starts eating*)

JORDAN
Me too.
(*He opens the other lunch.*)
And your mom made peanut butter
and jelly. Great.
You know, there's enough in that
Lunch-munchie for both of us.
(*Darby ignores him*)
At least give me the 50 cents back.

Darby thinks about it, then slides only one
of the quarters over. Jordan looks at his
sandwich, and half of his money; sighs. He
made a bad trade.

JORDAN
I stink at gambling.

"I'll Say A Word..."

LINDSEY and ALLISON are trying to do their homework, but just aren't into it...

> LINDSEY
> Hey, let's play a game. A word game.

> ALLISON
> I really need to get this done...

> LINDSEY
> Come on! Here's the game: I'll say something, and you say the first word that comes to your mind.

> ALLISON
> How do I know if I got it right?

> LINDSEY
> There's no right or wrong, you just play.

> ALLISON
> Alright.

> LINDSEY
> Ok. First word: "cat".

> ALLISON
> Ping pong.

LINDSEY
What? That doesn't make any sense.

ALLISON
You said there wasn't any right or
wrong.

LINDSEY
There's no right or wrong, but there's
'weird'. And that was weird.

ALLISON
Wait, you make up the rules and then
get bossy with me when I don't play
the way you want? Go play by
yourself; I have homework to do.

She buries herself in her book. A pause.

LINDSEY
Ok, you don't have to get mad. It's
just a game. I said I was sorry.

ALLISON
Actually you didn't. And by the way,
my cat sleeps on the ping-pong table

She waves 'good-bye', not looking up.
Lindsay's face drops as she leaves.

© Bo Kane

"Try"

JACKIE is drawing on a piece of heavy
paper when TAYLOR walks up.

TAYLOR
What'cha doing?

JACKIE
Making my mother a Mother's Day
card.

TAYLOR
You're making it? Wow. Did you
draw this?

JACKIE
Yeah. Now I'll write a little rhyme or
something. You should try it.

TAYLOR
No, I'm not really good at drawing.
Or rhyming. Or … anything.

JACKIE
Yes you are.

TAYLOR
No, it's true. I'm kind-of good at a
lot of things, but I'm not really good
at … anything.

She holds up the pen, offering it to him.

> JACKIE
>
> Try.

> TAYLOR
>
> No, I can't. I'll just buy her a card.

> JACKIE
>
> Try.   Stop making excuses and 'try'.

> TAYLOR
>
> I don't know…

> JACKIE
>
> And you'll never know. If you don't try. Ok?

> TAYLOR
>
> Ok. I'll try.

She leaves. He picks up the pen and paper, and, muttering to himself ….

> TAYLOR (cont'd)
>
> 'Thank you Mom, for all you do..
> I love it when you make a stew'….

Expression: *'Hey, I'm kinda good at this.'*

"Famous"

TRACY glides in singing while HILARY
sits paging through a dictionary...

TRACY
(singing)
Sen-sational! Famous and sen-
sational. I'm gonna be hotter than
hot! Like it or not! Sen-sational!

HILARY
Hey. Hot stuff. Can you sing "Far,
far away"?

TRACY
I'm not sure I .... oh, I get it. You're
clever. When I'm a star will you
write stuff like that for me? Because I
AM going to be famous.

HILARY
Good for you.

TRACY
Oh, don't be jealous. We'll still be
friends when I have thousands of
adoring fans. I'll be on tv,
photographers will be taking my
picture everywhere...

HILARY
Yeah. People will be running after
'the star', cameras clicking, and …
they might take bad pictures of you on
purpose. And post 'em.

Tracy considers this. Then, …

TRACY
Nah. Besides, I can have my agent
photo-shop them for me. Think of
it, Hilary—you can write songs for a
famous singer. Won't it be great?!

HILARY
Oh, yeah. Great.

TRACY
(dancing away, singing)
I'm going to be a shining star. Super
hot, brightest star in the galaxy…

Tracy dances away. Hilary pages through
her dictionary.

HILARY
Hmm. Star: noun. A ball of gas held
together by its own gravity. Yep.

Closes the book, smiles.

"Poetry: Good For The Heart"

MAE is looking through a poetry book when ANDREW walks in.

ANDREW
What'cha doing?

MAE
I have to find a poem to read in class. Do you know any poems?

ANDREW
Sure. *'Beans beans, they're good for your heart, the more you eat, the more you... '*

MAE
Not that kind!! I need one that will move people, inspire them.

ANDREW
Inspire them to do what?

MAE
I'm not sure... Wait, here's one"

"I wish I could take those words back. Could put them back in my mouth. I was trying to be funny, but it came out mean. And suddenly things went south.
(more)

132

MAE (cont'd)

"Once the genie is out of the
bottle, it's hard for him to come
back. So from now on I'll
watch my words. And
cut my friends some slack."

ANDREW
That's pretty good; words can hurt,
and … whatever else you said.
But hey, there's also a second one of
mine: *'Beans, beans the musical*
fruit. The more you eat, the…'

MAE
Stop it! Enough about beans! Here,
Stinky, read some <u>real</u> poetry.

She throws the book at him and exits.

ANDREW
'The more you eat, the more you
toot'. Heh, heh. Never gets old.

"The Tryout"

JAKE and SARAH walk out of school.

SARAH
What's going on? You ok?

JAKE
Aw, my dad is making me try out
for baseball. On Saturday.

SARAH
That's great. My dad loves baseball
too.

JAKE
Well I don't. I'm no good at it. I'm
gonna get roasted out there.

SARAH
No you're not. I'll bet you're good
at baseball. Have you been to the
batting cage?

JAKE
No, that's just it. My dad hasn't had
any time to help me; he just wants me
to be good at it because he was good.
But he's in Dallas until Friday.

SARAH

Want me to ask my dad to take us?
He loves to hit in the batting cage.

JAKE

You've been to the batting cage?

SARAH

Lots of times. I'll bet my dad would
love to help you out. Let's go tonight.
He'll help you hit, and afterwards we
can go to Dairy Queen.

JAKE

Ok.

Jake is stunned with gratitude.

SARAH

I'll call you when my dad gets home.

JAKE

Great. Thanks.

She waves, walks away. Jake's expression
changes from afraid to anticipation. He
pretends he's facing a pitcher, swings at a
fastball and hits an air double.

"Life's Not Fair"

Keegan and Catie have moved to a new
house, but still have to share a room.

CATIE
So when you're in my room, you do
what I tell you to do. Got it?

KEEGAN
Why do I have to listen to you? It's
my room too.

CATIE
Because I'm older and that's the way
it is.

KEEGAN
That's not fair!

CATIE
No, life's not fair. Just one of the
many things I'll be teaching you.
Now pick up my books and pens and
put them on my desk. Neatly.

Keegan bends down and picks up all of
Catie's things, steps toward the desk, then
HOLDS THE BOOKS UP HIGH and
DROPS THEM all over the floor.

KEEGAN
Oops.

Keegan exits with a smirk. Catie reacts.

*"Whether he's playing big and broad, or
small and understated, an actor has to be ...*
believable."

- Bo Kane

"Unfriended"

ELIZABETH and KARI are sitting in a McDonald's.

> BETH
>
> I haven't seen Vanessa in a while, have you?

> KARI
>
> No, we're not friends anymore.

> BETH
>
> Why? What happened?

> KARI
>
> I don't know. Some of us went to the concert at the mall and we didn't invite her, and she flipped out on me. So, I unfriended her.

> BETH
>
> Oh... When was that?

> KARI
>
> Last week; what difference does it make? She got all weird; I don't need that...
> *(looks at Beth's knowing face)*
> What?

BETH

Vanessa's brother left home about a
week ago. After her mom moved her
grandmother in, I guess her brother
couldn't take it, so he moved out.
And you know how she idolizes her
big brother.

KARI

Oh no. I didn't even ask her about…
Her life was crazy and I told her to
'just chill'. This is terrible.

BETH

You didn't know.

KARI

Because I didn't ask. I was only
thinking of myself. I'm a horrible
person.

She buries her head in her hands.

BETH

Well, you did kick her when she was
down. I mean, when somebody flips
out for no reason, instead of getting
mad, you might be curious about, you
know …

Kari lifts her head, stares at Beth.

KARI

Are you done?

BETH

Yep.

KARI

Ok. I have to fix this. I will friend
her again and say I'm sorry. And then
I'll go see her.

She pulls out her phone and types.

BETH

You know ... you didn't invite **me** to
the concert at the mall either.

KARI

Ooh. Sorry. ... Uh, here, have some
of my fries. We good?

BETH

We're cool.

She eats the fries as Kari tries to make
amends.

"Charity Begins At Home"

CHRIS is stuffing clothing into a sack when WILL enters his house.

> WILL
> Hey, Chris, you want to go over to the skate park?

> CHRIS
> Yeah, soon as I finish putting these shirts and stuff in the giveaway bag.

> WILL
> (looks at the clothes)
> This stuff?

> CHRIS
> Yeah. I don't really wear these anymore. And those don't fit me, so we're giving them to charity.
> They'll fit somebody.

> WILL
> (holding up a shirt)
> Bro, I don't know anybody who can't afford a shirt. Especially a used one.

> CHRIS
> Seriously? Okay, well, your parents
> (more)

CHRIS (cont'd)
both went to college, and my dad
became an engineer in the Navy; but
some kids don't have that. Some
don't even have a dad.

WILL
Hmf. Whose fault is that?

Chris exhales, tries to explain....

CHRIS
Last time I was there, a little boy
walked in with his mom. He was
maybe six; skinny kid with big eyes,
and he was so happy to get the
clothes they gave him. And he got an
old baseball glove, and his mom got
some soup and rice and ... you could
see they really needed it.

So I don't know whose fault it was;
but I know this---it wasn't that little
boy's fault.

He throws the bag over his shoulder.

CHRIS (cont'd)
Come on. I'll leave this for my mom
and we'll go skate.

142

WILL
Hey, wait. You know, ... um, I've
got some old stuff I don't wear
anymore too. When's your mom
going?

Will shrugs a *'ok, you convinced me'*. Chris
is pleasantly surprised.

CHRIS
Tomorrow. Let's go get your stuff.

They exit.

Curses! Cursive!"

MO is writing/crossing out words and
getting frustrated when HARLEY comes up.

MO
Arrgghh!! This is so dumb.

HARLEY
What are you doing?

MO
Cursive. I print the line, then I have
to "write" it.

HARLEY
Our teacher doesn't use cursive.

MO
Mrs. Lane showed us the Declaration
of Independence and it has all these
names written at the bottom. Then
she asked how many of us knew how
to write our name. Zero. No one in
our class knew how to sign their
name. So now we're learning cursive.

HARLEY
Well, when you get old you have to
sign your name all the time. My
dad's a lawyer and he has people sign
their name every day.

MO
Can you sign your name?

HARLEY
Yeah. My signature is the only thing
I can write, but yeah.

MO
Hmmm…my own signature. Mo
Leahy.
(writes in the air)
Like that Hancock guy. Ok, maybe
this won't be so bad.

Mo goes back to 'writing'. Harley leans
over and looks at the paper.

HARLEY
Um, I think that loop goes on the
other side.

MO
Arrgghh!!

Mo crosses it out again.

© Bo Kane

"Splash Attack"

It's 1965 at the public swimming pool.
BOB got the whistle from the Lifeguard, and
is sitting on the 'time-out' bench. GREG:

GREG
I've been looking for you, Bob. What
did you do?

BOB
Aw, I snuck up on Sue and splashed
her in the face and her friend went
whining to the Lifeguard.

Greg drops his smile immediately.

GREG
Whoa. You're the one...

BOB
One what? I was just ...

GREG
(interrupting)
She's over by the concession stand
with an ice pack on her eye. You
didn't just splash her, you whacked
her eye.

BOB
I was only ... it was an accident. I
didn't mean to hurt her.

GREG

Well, you did. And all her friends are mad at you too. You gotta go apologize.

BOB

I can't. They won't let me leave this bench for 15 more minutes.

GREG

No good. You gotta go now and tell her you're sorry. Hey – I'll put this towel over my head and sit here; the lifeguard will think it's you. Go.

BOB

Can I just hit my head with a brick instead? ... Ok, you're right. I'll be right back.

They switch places.

GREG

Don't make it worse.

Bob begins his march to humiliation.

"Splash Attack 2"

SUE holds her hand over her injured eye.
ANGIE holds an ice cream cone in one
hand, peeks through Sue's fingers.

> ANGIE
> It doesn't look too bad. I think the
> cold pack helped. I can't believe he
> hit you like that

> SUE
> He didn't mean to hit me; I think he
> just meant to splash me and he got too
> close.

> ANGIE
> Boys are so stupid sometimes. Most
> of the time.

> BOB (O.S.)
> Yeah. We are.

They turn, surprised to see him.

> BOB (cont'd)
> I'm sorry, Susie.

> ANGIE
> You should be! You almost poked
> her eye out!

Sue gives her a tap to 'cool it'.

> SUE
> It'll be alright.

> BOB
> I didn't mean to touch you, I just …
> I wish I could make it up to you.

Sue looks forgiving. Bob glances away, sees Angie's ice cream.

> BOB (cont'd)
> Angie, I'll give you the money for this in a minute.

Bob scoops the ice cream out of Angie's cone, puts it in Sue's hand. He leans his face forward.

> BOB
> Go ahead, hit me with it.

> SUE
> No, I'm not going to hit you.

> ANGIE
> I'll hit him!

BOB
Go ahead. It'll make you feel better.
Really.

Sue thinks about it, looks like she won't do
it. Then winds up and SMASHES the ice
cream right in Bob's face. Every kid laughs,
even Angie. Bob doesn't try to clean it off;
takes his punishment with a half-smile.

SUE
You're right. I do feel better.

BOB
Told ya. I really am sorry.
*(wipes his eye, it stings. Looks
at Angie)*
Salted Caramel? Really?

ANGIE
Aww, does it sting?

They all laugh. He gets a towel, waves
good-bye.

NOTE: *You can ball up the middle of a
slice of bread to use as the ice cream.*

© Bo Kane

NOTES FROM THE COACH

* In *"Charity Begins At Home"* (pg 141) Will has a breakthrough. Before this day, he couldn't imagine someone not having enough money to buy new clothes. Chris has made him realize how lucky he is.

* Check out the Declaration of Independence for *"Curses! Cursive!"* (144) Take a look at those signatures.

* *"Splash Attack 1 & 2"* (146) deal with Bob's mistake, and how to correct it. He runs through denial, confusion, and then owning up. While Sue is willing to forgive, Angie is a fireball; have fun with her.

* *"Dancin' Fool"* (pg. 152) only requires just a few easy dance steps. You can use the one in the scene or make up your own.

* In *"Funeral Party"* (154) Morgan not only tells the story of her late grandfather, but **shows** us how he had fun (kicking the ball, sneaking the ice cream). From the heart.

* *"Special Kid"* (156) requires some care to make Riley a character, not a caricature. He feels the pressure, but doesn't lose his sense of humor. And he really appreciates Sam; she (or he) is the friend we all want.

* At one point in *"...Zoo"* (pg 158) Katie interrupts Cody. Cody won't just stop, he'll add a 'you know' or stammer until she breaks in. Timing.

"Dancin' Fool"

DECLAN sees Marley in the hallway.

DECLAN

Marley! Just the girl I was looking for.

MARLEY

Ooh, I don't like the sound of that. What do you want, Declan?

DECLAN

I'm trying out for the musical, and I need some help.

MARLEY

Oh. That's not as bad as I thought it would be... What do you need?

DECLAN

I have a monologue, but I also need to show them some dancing --- which I've never done. But you're a good dancer; could you show me a few easy steps? Emphasis on "easy".

MARLEY

Just a few steps? Sure. How about a grapevine?

He looks at her like she just spoke Swahili.

>   MARLEY (cont'd)
> Here, stand next to me and follow.
> We'll go left and then come back.
> Side step, behind, side and tap. So:
> side, behind, side and tap.
> And then we go back.

She does it with him a couple of times, back and forth. Trevor slowly untangles his feet and gets it. She tells him *"that's it, no-- in front, behind; good, you're getting it! Keep your head up."* He can even put a small dip into it. Finally …

>   DECLAN
> This is great, Marley, thanks a lot.

>   MARLEY
> You're welcome. Break a leg.

Marley walks on.

>   DECLAN
> Hey Marley! What did you think I wanted when I first walked up?

>   MARLEY
> Never mind.

He watches her go. Hmmm …

"Funeral Party"

QUINN sees MORGAN at the mall.

QUINN
Morgan! Didn't see you at band this weekend. Where were you?

MORGAN
At my grandpa's funeral.

QUINN
Oh. Sorry...I didn't know. Are you ok? Must've been really sad, huh?

MORGAN
I thought it would be, and my mom was really sad on the way there. But when we got there it was more like a party than a funeral. Everyone was telling stories about my grandpa and laughing and joking.

QUINN
Really? Even at the funeral?

MORGAN
Yeah. My grandpa was a good guy. The priest talked about how when they played golf together my grandpa would always 'kick' his ball out of the sand trap. *(more)*

MORGAN

And when the priest would catch him
and say *"ahem!"* Grandpa would look
at his ball all surprised and yell, *"It's
a miracle!"*
Everybody laughed at that one.

QUINN

I've never been to a funeral like that.
Most of the time everyone is crying.

MORGAN

My grandpa didn't want that. He
used to take me to the park and to
Dairy Queen. But if you looked the
other way, he would bite off the top of
your ice cream and then look innocent
like this:
          (rolls eyes away and whistles)
And then he'd laugh and buy me
another one.

QUINN

He sounds like a fun grandpa.

MORGAN

He was...I'm really gonna miss him.

"Special Kid"

RILEY, a former special ed student (now in regular class) looks miserable as OLIVIA approaches.

OLIVIA
Hey Riley, how are you doing? You ok?

RILEY
No. We just had a test in math. I didn't do too well. Some kids saw my grade. uuggghh!

OLIVIA
It's ok, don't get mad at yourself. We all get a lousy grade once in a while.

RILEY
I didn't like it when they made fun of me. 'Specially Drake. He's mean.

OLIVIA
I know. I'm sorry you got a bad grade, but you knew it would be tougher this year, right? And you're doing really well in regular school; it took a lot of guts to be here with all of those Drakes and …probably Marco too, right?

RILEY

Marco was even worse. He kept
calling me 'tardo'. I wish I could beat
him up.

OLIVIA

Not that he doesn't deserve it, but
you're better than that. Try not to pay
attention to them, and next time you
have a hard test coming up, ask the
teacher for some help. And if that
doesn't work, I'll help you.

RILEY
(small smile)
Would you beat up Marco for me?

OLIVIA

No problem. I'll tear him apart for
ya. (*smiles*) Nah, he'd kick my butt.
Let him be a jerk, we'll just work a
little harder. I gotta go. Text me if
you need help. Bye.

RILEY

Thanks. You're the best.

OLIVIA

Glad you noticed.

© Bo Kane

"It's All Happening At The Zoo"

CODY and KATIE are leaving school.

KATIE
Woo-hoo! We have tomorrow off.
What are you going to do?

CODY
Same thing I always do---play video
games.

KATIE
What kind of video games?

CODY
"Assassin's Mission", where you
shoot people, and "Danger-Zone",
where you ..

KATIE
(interrupts)
Shoot people, got it. We're going to
the zoo tomorrow. Zeke is coming,
and my cousin. Wanna go?

CODY
The zoo? What's at the zoo?

KATIE
Seriously?

CODY

I mean, what's *interesting* at the zoo?

KATIE

Last time we were there the elephants
were swimming by us with these huge
toys, and we made faces on the glass
and I swear they were laughing at us.
And the chimps are always funny.

CODY

I don't know ...

KATIE

And the giraffes had a baby; I want to
see how big it is now. Their tongues
are purple and super long. Well, have
fun shooting people. See you later.

CODY

Ok. ... uh, wait. I'll probably finish
conquering the Templars tonight. I
could go with you, if you want.

KATIE

Sure! Pick you up at 9. Bring a
couple of dollars for giraffe food; they
eat right out of your hand.

She flicks her eyebrows, smiles, and exits.

"Frame The Star"

McKENNA sees AIDEN at lunch….

McKENNA
Hey Aiden, I'm making a YouTube video! Want to be in it?

AIDEN
What's it about?

McKENNA
I don't know yet. But it has to be **funny** or it won't get lots of views. Maybe a funny prank. Can you act?

AIDEN
Not really.

McKENNA
Sing? Dance?

AIDEN
Not even close. Thanks anyway. Good luck.

McKENNA
Wait! You can hit and catch a baseball; that means you have good eyes. And you're strong…you're my cameraman!

> AIDEN
>
> What? McKenna, the only camera
> I've ever used is my phone.

> McKENNA
>
> Don't worry. I'll put it on auto-focus.
> Just frame the shot and make me look
> good. Kidding! I'll handle that part.
> Ok, I'm the actress, so all I need is a
> story, a script, some extras, and props.
> Easy peasy. It'll be great!

She starts to go, then turns back.

> McKENNA (cont'd)
>
> By the way, we start shooting
> tomorrow!

> AIDEN
>
> Tomorrow!?!
> *(she's gone)*
> O-kay. I'm a cameraman. It'll be
> funny alright.

He gets up, frames an imaginary shot with
his fingers, then thinks back with a grin...

> AIDEN (cont'd)
>
> She called me 'strong'.

"Rumor Has It"

KELLY walks up to the hallway locker, feels the stares from the other kids. ANDY comes up.

> KELLY
>
> What's going on?

> ANDY
>
> Everybody's talking about you. Are you ok?

> KELLY
>
> Yeah. Why?

Kelly looks again at the curious kids.

> ANDY
>
> We heard about the fight. And we thought you might be injured.

> KELLY
>
> Injured? What fight?

> ANDY
>
> The fight! Your fight! Oh, ok, sorry, you don't want to talk about it.

> KELLY
>
> I can't talk about it, because I don't know what you're talking about.

ANDY

You and your brother! The other
night. Maxy walked by your house
and heard everything. Did your
brother … did he go to jail?

KELLY

No, he went to the theater.

ANDY

They jailed him in a theater?!

KELLY

No! He got a part in a play at the
Starlight; he's playing a tough juvey
kid who gets in a fight. I was just
helping him rehearse. I guess next
time we better close the windows.

ANDY

Whoa. And that rumor spread fast!
EVERYBODY thinks you were in a
fight. I guess we better tell them …

KELLY

No wait; hold on. I was in a fight...
and came out without a scratch.
Let's let it go. This could be good.

Devious smiles as they walk off.

"Cereal Prankster"

The OLDER SISTER sits at breakfast with her YOUNGER BROTHER.

BROTHER
Hey, why do you get the cereal with the berries in it, and I only get the plain flakes? ... I wanted pancakes.

SISTER
Mom doesn't have time to make you pancakes, she's going to work. And there's only one bowl of berry cereal left and it's mine.

BROTHER
Aww.

SISTER
And no whining. When mom's gone I'm in charge: you do what I tell you to do, eat what I tell you to eat and tell me everything that's going on, good or bad. You report to me, got it?

BROTHER
I guess so. Well, here's my report: there's a lotta bugs in your closet.

SISTER
What!?!

BROTHER

I guess you dropped a chip on the floor. There's lots of bugs. Way in the back too.

The Big sister jumps up

SISTER

My new shoes! Ahh! I hate bugs!

She RUNS out. He slides her bowl of cereal over to his side. Takes a bite.

BROTHER

That was too easy.

Eats with a smile.

© Bo Kane

"Halloween"

COOPER is at the kitchen table looking at pictures of costumes when GIGI enters.

COOPER
What are you going to be for Halloween?

GIGI
Halloween is two months away.

COOPER
Right! Can't wait. So what's gonna be your costume?

Gigi grabs some grapes and sits with him.

GIGI
I don't know. I just know I'm not going to be 'sweet'---no Tinkerbelles. This year I want to scare people.

COOPER
When I said I want to be scary, Dad said '*go as the evening news.*' Not sure what that means. Hey, I can be a vulture with nasty wings, and hang a dead squirrel from my claws!

GIGI
Ycch! That's gross, not scary.

COOPER
Not a real squirrel. A fake one.
Ooh, how about this?---a SWAT guy!
I could get a water gun, storm up to
the porch and yell *"Trick or Treat!*
Now! Move! Move! Fire in the hole!"

GIGI
You'll get a lot of doors slammed in
your face. I saw this shop that had
zombie masks; I could get one and put
fake blood over my eye … with my
severed tongue hanging …

COOPER
(interrupts)
Mom will NEVER let you do that.

GIGI
She won't let you be a squirrel-
killing vulture either. *(sigh)* I guess
we'll end up being Han Solo and
Princess Leia again.

COOPER
I hope not. *(pause)* But if we do, this
year I'M Han Solo!

He follows her out.

"What Do You Want To Be?"

TRE and DAKOTA are sitting on a school ledge, waiting for their parents to get them.

DAKOTA
Our teacher is making us write 'what we want to be' when we grow up.

TRE
Mr. Davis gave us that same assignment. When I was in kindergarten, I wrote that I wanted to be a fireman or a motorcycle cop because they got to drive really fast. But now I think it should be more important.

DAKOTA
Those are pretty important, and exciting. I was going to write that I'd be a lawyer like my dad. But that's not too exciting. Maybe I should say that I'm going to be a spy.
(foreign accent)
"I will uncover your secrets. One way ... or another."

TRE
"Put him on the rack, Natasha. He will talk. Heh-heh." Being a spy could be cool. Now, for me ...what would be important and exciting?

TRE (cont'd)
What about an astronaut? I could go
to Mars in a spaceship!

DAKOTA
I saw astronaut training in science. I
think you'd throw up in that 'vomit
comet' that they spin you around in.
Maybe you were right the first time;
being a policeman is important and
exciting. But it's dangerous.
(sees her Mom arrive)
Gotta go.
(starts to leave, then …
foreign accent)
"Good bye, and, good luck".

She's gone.

TRE
(to himself)
Yeah. She's right. I'd barf in the
rocket. Motorcycle cop it is.

He sees his mother drive up and runs out.

© Bo Kane

"Change of Climate"

Younger BROTHER is working on a poster board science project when his SISTER approaches.

> SISTER
> Is that your science project?

> BROTHER
> Yeah. I'm almost done. It's about climate change.

> SISTER
> You put the sun in the wrong spot. Put it over here.

She picks up the sun and re-tapes it to a different spot on the board.

> BROTHER
> What are you doing? That's where it goes!

> SISTER
> No, it doesn't, and your glacier is too big on top. It's supposed to be small, and the bottom bigger…

> BROTHER
> Just leave it alone. The sun goes back over here and the glacier is fine.

SISTER

Go ahead, put it there. I'm right and
you're wrong, but go ahead. Get a
"C" if you want to. F-Y-I, I never got
a "C" in any subject. Ever.

BROTHER

That's because teachers don't grade
on mean-ness. They don't care that
you're a *"I'm smarter than you"* pain
in the neck.
> (picks up his stuff)

They don't care; but the rest of us do.

He leaves.

SISTER

I'm still right!

He's gone; she's alone. She thinks about it:
Am I too bossy? Do I <u>only</u> want to be right?
Hmmm. (Does she take it to heart, or not
care at all? Try different final moments.)

NOTE: For the 'moveable' sun, try a
yellow post-it note.

© Bo Kane

"I Bet You're Right"

EMILY leans against her locker, unable to move, when MICHAEL sees her.

MICHAEL
Hey, Em. You okay?

EMILY
No. I just saw this accident and it kind of freaked me out. 'Cause I saw it in my head and then it happened.

MICHAEL
You saw it...before it happened?
Whoa. Was it a bad accident?

EMILY
No, just a "bang!-crunch!" at the traffic light. Right in front of me.

MICHAEL
Were you in the street?

EMILY
No, I was riding in the car next to the lady who was texting and drinking coffee -- as she was driving! For like a mile! I said out loud: *"I bet she gets into an accident."*
And a half mile later she hit this car at the stoplight. It's like I caused it.

MICHAEL
She wasn't paying attention. You didn't say you HOPED she'd hit someone or you WISHED she'd get into an accident.

EMILY
I said 'I bet'.

MICHAEL
Doesn't count. Unless you used your super telekinetic power to MAKE it happen, it was her stupid texting and driving that caused it. Not you. I BET she doesn't do that again.

EMILY
You're right; it had nothing to do with me. I don't know why I feel guilty.

Michael picks up a pencil like a wand…

MICHAEL
My wizardry will enter your brain. Lose the guilt! Feel good again! Voila'!

She smiles a 'thank you'

MICHAEL (cont'd)
Magic at a discount. 5 bucks please.

© Bo Kane

173

"Life Lessons"

MILEY (the older sibling) and CASEY are moving into their Dad's house for the weekend, and a new *shared* bedroom.

> MILEY
> It doesn't thrill me either, but here's how it's gonna be...when you're in my room, you do what I tell you to do. Got it?

> CASEY
> Why do I have to listen to you? It's my room too.

> MILEY
> Because I'm older and that's the way it is.

> CASEY
> That's not fair!

> MILEY
> No, life's not fair. Just one of the many things I'll be teaching you. So to pay me back for my brilliant instruction, you're on clean-up crew. Pick up my school books and put them on my bookshelf.

Casey stalls, thinks...then picks up the stack of books, steps toward the bookcase, holds the books high in the air .... then DROPS THEM with a thud.

CASEY

Ooops.

Casey exits with a smirk. Miley reacts.

"If you get an impulse in a scene, no matter how wrong it seems, follow the impulse. It might be something. And if it ain't --- take two!"

- Jack Nicholson

NOTES FROM THE COACH

* In *"Frame The Star"* (160) Aiden can't /
doesn't say 'no' but does he really want to?
His re-actions are very important. And, as
self-absorbed as McKenna is, she has
energetic charm.

* *"Rumor Has It"* (162) has a touch of French
farce. Something was heard out of context
and taken to an extreme.

* Let's try to make sure our *"Cereal
Prankster"* (pg 164) doesn't give away his
new plan too soon. Be very sincere about
the bugs (that don't exist).

* In *"Change of Climate"* (pg 170) it may be
the 100th time that his sister has been bossy
and 'know-it-all' and he's had it. Feel like
you can show the passion. How does the
sister feel at the end? Show us.

* Emily has a big emotional arc in *"I Bet
You're Right"* (pg 172). A bit in shock, to
frustrated guilt, to feeling blameless, then
good. Michael is a good friend, and has fun
with his 'magical' flair (which could also be
like a televangelist with his hand on her
head shouting "heal!")

* In *"Life Lessons"* (174) the reactions are
just as important as the lines. In the end, did
Miley learn something when Casey
wouldn't take her orders? Or will she put
the hammer down even harder? Show us.

Acting Scenes with Adults

"Cat Tale"

An upset Austin runs in with a bleeding scratch on his arm.

AUSTIN
Mom! Look at this—that stupid cat scratched me!

MOM
Oh, dear. What cat?

AUSTIN
That big one! You know … the one from down the block.

MOM
What were you doing to it?

AUSTIN
Nothing!

MOM
Did you step on its tail, or hit it …?

AUSTIN
No, I wasn't doing anything. It just reached out and bit me.

MOM
Hold it. A moment ago, you said it scratched you.

He stands frozen, as she arches her eyebrow.

                MOM (cont'd)
I'm going to go get some band-aids,
and you're going to get your story
straight.

She comes back to an embarrassed Austin.

                MOM (cont'd)
Austin, what happened to your arm?

                AUSTIN
Jesse and me found some big sticks
and were sword-fighting.
        (He holds out his arm)
I'm sorry...

                MOM
I trust you to tell me the truth.
Always.

                AUSTIN
I will. Sorry mom.

                MOM
Next time, use pool noodles.

From embarrassed to *'that's a great idea.'*

                            © Bo Kane

179

"Note From Teacher"

ERIN (Aaron) carries an envelope into the kitchen. Looks at Dad.

> ERIN
> They want you to read this note and sign it. It's from my teacher.

> DAD
> Ok. Is it a good note, or a bad one?

> ERIN
> I don't know.

> DAD
> (eyebrows arched)
> *Ahem.*

> ERIN
> It's a bad one.

Erin (Aaron) sheepishly hands over the note. Then …

> ERIN (cont'd)
> But in my defense … all the kids thought I was funny!

"Poor Side Of Town"

ELLE gets in the car seat, slumps, frowning.

                    ELLE
          Aarrgghh! Ok, I'm done.
          Can we go?

                    MOM
          Should I even ask?

                    ELLE
          Lindsey told everyone she's going to
          the New York Dance Academy this
          summer.   **I** wanted to do that.

                    MOM
          And I told you, we can't afford that
          one. It's incredibly expensive.

                    ELLE
          I'm a better dancer than she is. I'll
          pay you back.

                    MOM
          We don't have the tuition, period.
          Besides, Webster college has a great
          day camp right here.

                    ELLE
          Thrilling.

MOM

Stop it. You know I'd like to send
you to New York. I can't. I'm sorry.
'It's not about having what you want,
it's about wanting what you've got.'
Sheryl Crow.

ELLE

I'm supposed to be happy we're poor?

MOM

You're supposed to be happy, period.
We have enough to send you to the
camp here, but not enough to send
you to New York. Sorry.

ELLE

Can't you borrow it?

She sees the answer is 'no'. Sighs and looks
out the car window. After a pause ...

MOM

Would a smoothie help?

ELLE

You sure we can afford it?

Mom is hurt by that. Her eyes get wet and
she stares straight ahead as she drives on.

182

ELLE (cont'd)
Hey, I'm sorry. Mom, the Juice It Up
is back that way.
(pause)
Mom, I didn't mean it. I shouldn't
have said that. Mom?

Mom wipes her eye.

MOM
Ok. You want a smoothie?

ELLE
No. I just want to take back what I
said. I'm really sorry.

NOTES FROM THE COACH

* In *"Cat Tale"* (178) Austin really sells
  his story ... mad and animated, until ...
  he slips up. He then is truly sorry, a
  complete change of emotion. Mom gives
  him not only a pass, but a good idea.
  Austin's face should show that appreciation.

* We've all complained and made
  someone feel badly for something out
  of their control, and in *"Poor Side Of
  Town"* (pg 181) Elle does just that.
  Emotional scene.

* At the end of *"Daddy-Tea"* (pg 186)
  there is an opportunity to eliminate
  Sophie's last line, and let Dad and Sophie
  ad-lib. Dad could ask why she was upset
  earlier, what he should get Mommy for their
  anniversary, where should they go on
  vacation, etc. Good chance to improv.

* In *"Kale and Ice Cream"* (188) Tara has a
  tiny window high up in her door to talk
  through, and the stool helps her be bolder
  than she might have been.

* In *"Racing With The Wind"* (187) Colby and
  his mother are not off by themselves. Play
  that there are others around.

* In *"Money For Nothing"* (190) our mom's
  sass will help Stacy re-act; so, Mom, give it
  to her. Stacy can re-act to the hiding place,
  then the slobber.

"Daddy Rule Book – Football"

RUBEN sees his dad come through the door.

> **RUBEN**
> Hey Dad! You have to play football
> with me.

> **DAD**
> I do?

> **RUBEN**
> Yeah. It's in the Daddy Rule Book.
> It says that if you play with me, and I
> grow up to be a famous football
> player, you can watch me on tv.

> **DAD**
> It says all that, huh?

> **RUBEN**
> And because you played with me,
> when I grow up and make millions of
> dollars playing football, I'll give you
> some.

> **DAD**
> Tell you what: Daddy Rule Book
> says 'no charge'. Let's go!

Ruben smiles, tosses him the football and
runs outside.

"Daddy Rule Book – Two For Tea"

SOPHIE has her tea party set, and sees Dad.

SOPHIE
Daddy! You have to play tea party
with me.

DAD
Is that right?

SOPHIE
Yep. It's in the Daddy Rule Book.
You get to sit right there and I'll pour
you some tea.

DAD
Ok. What kind of tea are we having?

SOPHIE
It's invisible tea. I made it myself.

She pours, and they clink cups and drink.

DAD
Cheers. Ahh. That's the best
invisible tea I've ever had.

EMMY
Thank you Daddy. You can go do
your work now if you want.

186

"Racing With The Wind"

COLBY is confident, stretching/warming up for a big race ...when he hears his mother.

COLBY
Mom! They don't want parents near the track.

MOM
You forgot your inhaler. Here…

COLBY
Mom! I didn't forget. I don't need it.

Colby pushes it back to her so no one sees it.

MOM
It will help you run better, believe me.
Just a couple of inhales.

COLBY
Fine. Could you stand there so
nobody sees me?
(inhales twice)

MOM
Very good. Ok, I'll be in the stands
by the other parents. You'll hear me.

COLBY
I'm sure I will... *(he runs off)*.

"Kale and Ice Cream"

After a knock on the door, TARA pulls a stool up to the small latched window (peephole). She sees a MAN on the porch with a carton of juice bottles.

MAN
Hello, young lady, is your mother home?

TARA
Maybe.

MAN
Maybe? You're not home alone are you?

TARA
I don't think that's any of your business. And I'm not supposed to talk to strangers. So goodbye.

MAN
Wait! I'm here to offer **your mother** a healthy food subscription that I think she'd be interested in. Our cleansing vegetable solutions help us stay fit and trim for only $4.99 per drink.

TARA

You want my mother to give you five bucks for that bottle of green stuff?

MAN

It's made from kale, asparagus and turmeric. All super foods.

TARA

Yuck! I'm going to **super** barf just hearing about it.
No. Thank. You. ... For five bucks we can get a great big carton of ice cream. The good kind!

She slams the little door and jumps off the stool.

© Bo Kane

"Money For Nothing"

Mom is in the kitchen when Stacy rushes in.

STACY
Mom! I need money for tonight—
everybody is going to the Crab Shack
and I can't go with no money. And
dad said I have to earn it, but I don't
have time to work for it. And he
won't just give it to me.

MOM
No, we earn our money around here.

STACY
He gives YOU money and you don't
work.

MOM
Ex-cuse me? You want to explain
that comment while I'm cooking, or
while I'm doing the laundry?

STACY
That's not what I meant, I mean you
don't GO to work.
I mean … uh; this isn't going the way
I wanted.

MOM
I'm sure it isn't.

190

MOM (cont'd)
Tell you what: I'll loan you the
money if you can name three things I
do for you.

STACY
I didn't mean it like that. Ok: dinner,
laundry, chauffeur, homework, nurse
… I could name a dozen. Sorry.

MOM
Thank you.

STACY
I'll just come home after the game.

MOM
I didn't say you couldn't go. I just
thought a little appreciation would be
nice. There's a twenty in the dog toy.

STACY
Thanks, Mom. The dog toy? I do
appreciate you. Really.
        (grabs it)
Ew, yuck, slobber. Thanks.

She extracts the hidden $20 and runs out.

"You Didn't Hear It From Me"

Tony sits in the Vice Principals office.

> VICE PRINCIPAL
> You could do us a big favor by telling us what you saw.

> TONY
> No way. I'm no snitch.

> VICE PRINCIPAL
> Okay. *(hits his phone button)* Martha, will you bring me some detention slips? Yes. Lots of them.

He glares at Tony. Tony hesitates, then…

> TONY
> Okay! Nathan pulled the alarm after Lexi took the tests.
> *(pause, worried)*
> But you didn't hear it from me.

He fidgets in his seat, not sure he made the right decision.

"Shorty" Scenes

Sometimes we get a part or an audition that isn't several pages long; it's only a few lines. We need to make those lines come to life in a short amount of time.
Let's practice.

"Target The Thief"

Two kids are shopping in Target when they see a man slip a watch into his pocket.

TRACY
Did you see that? The man over there.

SASHA
Did he just put that watch in his pocket?

TRACY
Yes, he's stealing it! Go tell the clerk.

SASHA
I'm not telling her, <u>you</u> go tell her.

TRACY
Sshh. He's looking at us. Be cool.

They freeze, big eyes; can't help but look. Maybe slink behind a shirt rack as they tiptoe away backwards. A good comic moment.

"Baby Birds"

MORGAN is looking out the window when
AUTRY enters.

> ### AUTRY
> What are you looking at?

> ### MORGAN
> That bird. It keeps flying away and
> coming back. I think there're babies
> in the nest.

> ### AUTRY
> She must be the mama bird. Yeah,
> look --- little heads are popping up.

> ### MORGAN
> Looks like she's going to feed the
> babies ....

They watch as the mama bird regurgitates
her food into the baby birds' mouths. Their
faces contort into ...

> ### AUTRY/MORGAN
> Yecchh!

"Right In The Can"

Two bored friends are slumped in their chairs watching tv. One grabs some paper, wads it up, and nods to a distant trashcan.

DREW
Watch this. Right in the can.

Lou looks at the distance, back at Drew…

LOU
You're never going to make that.

DREW
Wanna bet?

LOU
I'll bet you a nickel.

DREW
A nickel? That's all you've got? Ok, a nickel.

Drew shoots. 3 results to choose from:

Drew *makes it* (victory dance, Lou pays up)
Drew *misses* (dance and payment reversed)
    or
Drew *misses badly*, hits the sleeping cat who jumps up, knocks over a lamp and shatters it! *They gasp, then run out.*

"'Study' With Elaine"

ERIN and BAILEY are on their phones
looking for something to do.

>   ERIN
> Hey, let's call Elaine and ask her to
> come with us.

>   BAILEY
> Nah, her mom never lets her do
> anything that's fun. She's probably
> home studying math right now.

>   ERIN
> Yeah.
>   *(pause)*
> Hey, maybe we could ask her to come
> over here and "study".

>   BAILEY
> I don't want to st ... oh. Oh!
>   *(smiles; gets it)*
> Yeah. "Study".

Mischievous smiles, then call her.

"Bloodsucker"

JAKE sees his little brother MILES with his arm out, waiting for a mosquito to land.

> MILES
> Come on, little 'squito, try and bite me. See what happens.

SMACK. He swats it just as it lands.

> JAKE
> (messing with him)
> You killed it? It didn't even bite you.

> MILES
> It was going to. It was going to suck my blood. I did the world a favor.

> JAKE
> What if he was a daddy-bug? You just made his kid an orphan. Nice going, killer.

Jake walks away. Miles looks at the smashed bug, frowns for a second, then …

> MILES
> It was going to suck my blood!!
> Sorry. Jeesh.

> JAKE (O.S.)
> Killer.

"Spider In A Box"

BRADY brings AJ into his room.

> **BRADY**
> Want to see something really cool?

> **AJ**
> Ok, what is it?

Brady pulls out a shoebox.

> **BRADY**
> I caught this spider. A big, hairy one.
> You sure you want to see it?

> **AJ**
> I'm not afraid. Let's see it.

> **BRADY**
> Ok, not too close. Bum-da-da dum!

AJ cautiously looks in the box, then puts his palms up, like "I don't see anything." Brady looks into the now-empty box.

> **BRADY (cont'd)**
> Uh-oh…

[maybe at the end, Mom could scream from off-camera]

© Bo Kane

199

"Clever and Sneaky"

MORGAN is pacing, thinking…

MORGAN
Ok. We need someone clever,
smart, and just a little bit sneaky.

EVAN
Who can we get like that?

MORGAN
Me!

NOTE FROM THE COACH

In this brief bit, there are several ways to
say, *"little bit sneaky"*. We can stretch it
out, we can make it sound like an old movie
villain etc.
All three adjectives can have their own spin.
And, there are many ways to say that one
little syllable "me". It can have cheerleader-
like enthusiasm!! Or you can **think** the rest
of your phrase: 'Me. *[Duh.']*
Or, 'Me' .. *[who did you think I was talking
about?']*

 © Bo Kane

"Where's My Phone!"

Younger sibling CASEY is watching tv when the older sister EMMA rushes in.

> EMMA
>
> Have you seen my phone? I need it! My friends are trying to contact me … Where is that … I've been calling but it's on 'vibrate'. WHERE IS MY PHONE?!

Casey shrugs, Emma panics….

> EMMA (cont'd)
> Arrrgghh!

She rushes out. Casey picks up a magazine to reveal a vibrating phone.

> CASEY
> (imitates a previous
> conversation)
> 'Emma, would you please share some of your ice cream? You have the last of it.' *'No, I will not. I will be a stingy older sister.'*
> (looks at phone)
> Hmmm. 8 texts, group chat, 5 missed calls. Busy, busy, busy.
> (puts phone down)
> Coulda shared, but ya didn't.

"I Think I See The Problem"

LANA and CARLY are eating lunch.

LANA
That new boy Carter is cute. I'm trying to get him to like me but it just isn't working.

CARLY
You have to spend some time with him, get to know him.

LANA
I am. I asked him to play basketball with me yesterday.

CARLY
Good, that's a start. How did it go?

LANA
He couldn't handle my moves. I beat him like a drum.

CARLY
I think I see the problem…

"Higher Ground"

JULIAN is watching a video on his phone and laughing hysterically. SAGE, his sister, peers over his shoulder.

> SAGE
> Who's that?

> JULIAN
> He's an internet celebrity!

> SAGE
> Why? What does he do?

> JULIAN
> This!

> SAGE
> He falls flat on his face?

> JULIAN
> Yeah. Cool huh? He's my hero.

She leans in and watches some more. Pats him on the shoulder; as she **exits**...

> SAGE
> Set your sights a little higher.

> JULIAN
> Why? Whoa, hahahaha!

"Fine!"

Lucas is on one side of the (closed) door, Kari is on the other side.

KARI
Go away.

LUCAS
I'm sorry, alright?

KARI
No, it's not alright! Go away.

LUCAS
I didn't know. I said I'm sorry.

KARI
What part do you not understand?
The 'go' or the 'away'?!

LUCAS
Fine.

KARI
Fine!

The scene can end there, or add: 'How am I supposed to know that somethin' from a guy named Louie is valuable?' *"It was a Louis Vuitton!"* (He's a big-time designer).

"Strange Secret"

Charlie wears a mischievous look as he leans in and whispers to Lucy.

> CHARLIE
> What if I had a secret, a really good secret? And I was willing to tell it to my very good friend. For a dollar.

> LUCY
> A dollar? How good is the secret?

> CHARLIE
> Really good.   The best in the whole universe. For just a dollar.

Lucy thinks, pulls out a dollar. Holds it out but doesn't let go. Charlie also holds it....

> CHARLIE (cont'd)
> (*stage-whisper*)
> Cat pee glows under a black light.

> LUCY
> Yuck!! (*takes back the dollar*). And I don't even want to know how you know that!

She exits, muttering '*weirdo*.' He reacts. "What?"

"Chemo"

Ethan sits in his hospital bed wearing a
stocking cap. Every fiber in his body feels
miserable. He sees another kid; a patient
being wheeled in to his room.

ETHAN
Whatcha' in for? Chemo?

Ethan nods, knowingly, then struggles to sit
more upright. His voice is raspy.

ETHAN (cont'd)
Hate to tell you, but it only gets
worse.

"Do or do not. There is no 'try'."

- Yoda

"Crackers"

Shelby is eating crackers on a bench. When she sees Lucas sit down, she hides them.

> LUCAS
>
> Hey, whatcha' eatin'?

> SHELBY
>
> Nothing.

> LUCAS
>
> (peeks around her)
>
> Looks like somethin'. Somethin' good.

> SHELBY
>
> It's nothing.

> LUCAS
>
> Could I have some of that 'nothing'?

Shelby pulls her crackers out in full view. Thinks about sharing; about not sharing.

> SHELBY
>
> Oh, all right.

Sharing is caring.

"Glitter Dress"

Jada holds up her costume dress, looks at it. Hmm. Unsuspecting Dustin reads near her.

JADA
Now, if I could just get someone to *wear* the dress while I put the glitter on it ....

She slowly moves her eyes from the dress, to squarely on Dustin. He looks at Jada, looks at the dress. His EYES GET BIG as he realizes she wants him to put the dress on. Then... he's gone in a flash.

"Cookies"

Ava is hiding in the kitchen, peeks over the counter. She hears someone come in, ducks, hears the cookie jar open and close, then looks. Her eyes get big with surprise and shock, her mouth wide open. She waits a second, then runs (downstage).

AVA
Mom! Mom! I know who's been stealing all the cookies! It wasn't Miles; it was Daddy!

"Seaweed"

AJ is enjoying his (strange-looking) chips
when the bigger, meaner Biff grabs some of
AJ's chips and shoves them in his mouth.

> BIFF
> Hey, thanks for the chips, dude!

> AJ
> You like em? Wow. I didn't think
> you'd like *seaweed* chips.

Biff reacts to seaweed (maybe a spit-take).

*"Many kids are getting pretty good at the
'acting' part of the process. But we not only
acts ... we re-act and inter-act."*

- Bo Kane

"Conveniently Sick"

*Here is a scene that can be played a few different ways. When Quinn says "**I'm sick**" it can mean "I really am sick" or it can mean "I'm not sick, I'm going to play video games all day." Or, with a far different reading, "I'm not sick but I'm scared to go to school today because of a test, or because of a bully".*

Quinn is sitting slumped at the table when Mom enters.

MOM
Why aren't you getting ready for school?

QUINN
I'm not going to school.

MOM
Why not?

QUINN
I'm sick.

[optional last line: Mom says "Let's go to the doctor then; get dressed." Quinn reacts.]

"Daddy's Little Girl"

Sophie is lying in bed; the lights are about to go off when she makes a request…

> SOPHIE
> Daddy, could you leave the night light on?   And…could I have another blanket?

Dad smiles "yes" (or says it). As he goes…

> SOPHIE (cont'd)
> And a glass of water?

So far so good, so she tries one more.

> SOPHIE (cont'd)
> And some ice cream?

She smiles that little girl smile that has worked so often on her dad. We should see on her face (her reaction) if he's going to get her some, or if he's looking at her as though she asked for one thing too many.

"Siri-ous Homework"

Max is stumped on the homework assignment, then gets an idea. Grabs the iphone…

> **MAX**
> Siri, how many quarters in $4?

> **SIRI (V.O.)**
> There are 4 quarters in a dollar, so
> there are 16 quarters in 4 dollars.

> **MAX**
> Siri, if A times B equals 24, and A is
> 6, what is B?

> **SIRI (V.O.)**
> You should move the 6 to the other
> side of the equation, divide it
> yourself, and do your own homework
> from now on.

> **MAX**
> Come on! Really?!

> **SIRI (V.O.)**
> Siri-ously. Heh-heh.

Max wears a *"real funny"* expression as
he/she puts the phone down.

"Go Big, Or … "

NOAH wants to act, but doesn't want to do the traditional audition process.

NOAH

I really would like to play this part, but I hate to audition. The teacher and the student director sit and stare at you, and then: *'thank you'*.
And then you wait. But this part is good—the guy is mean and funny, so I really want to do it.
Wait! I know! I'll just go on stage and start yelling. No intro, no 'hi, how are you?' Just look off-stage like I was in an argument. Like **"Are you crazy?! There's NO WAY I'm going back and apologize!"**
They'll wonder what's going on until they figure out that I'm already in character doing the lines.
They'll either laugh or get mad. But they can't just sit there like this:
(mimics a stone-face)
I'm going for it. They might not pick me, but they won't forget me.

"Cup of Coffee"

BLAKE and CHARLEY see a cup of coffee.

> BLAKE
> Uh-oh, my dad left his cup of coffee.

> CHARLEY
> Ooh, I've seen him talk about his coffee.
> He's not going to be happy.

> BLAKE
> (mimics his Dad)
> That's my SuperPower! Makes me tough
> enough for the day's work.

They stare at the black liquid. Then …

> BLAKE
> Think it works?

> CHARLEY
> Let's try it.

They each take a big gulp. Tastes awful to them, but they try to be tough. Half of it still in their mouth …

> BLAKE
> It's good.

> CHARLEY
> Mm-hmm. I can feel it working. Gotta go.

> BLAKE
> Me too.

They take two steps away, then **spit-take!**

© Bo Kane

214

Acknowledgements

My biggest thanks and all my love to my wife, **Denise Loveday-Kane**, and our two kids, Austin and Makena. Denise advised all along the way, and the kids served as inspiration. Austin is now a working actor in TV and film; Makena has a film degree from UCLA and works for NFL Films.

The great artist **Tom Cain** designed the cover, front and back.

Tiber, Marleigh, Xander, Marley, Jenna, Anastasia, Bo, Arianwen, guest casting director, Aristotle, Sabine, Dylan, Eddie, Hannah Mae, Isaac, Scarlet, Lucas and Sara.

The monologues and scenes were tested by our students on-camera in a studio owned by Brian and Cinda Scott; our thanks to them.

And a huge thanks to all of those acting students, past and present, who come in to class every week with enthusiasm, talent, and a willingness to help the old coach with these scenes and monologues.

Bo Kane on '911 Lone Star'

"I love working with kids. Their eyes are bright, their laughs are genuine, and their world has endless possibility."

Also by Bo Kane -

"Acting Scenes and Monologues For Young Teens"

About The Author

As an actor, Bo Kane has worked in television shows such as *911 Lone Star*, Just Roll With It, *NCIS*, Criminal Minds, *Tacoma FD*, Jane The Virgin, *The Orville*, How To Get Away With Murder, *Colony*, Castle, *CSI: Miami,* Dexter, *90210*, Workaholics, *Outlaw*, Men Of A Certain Age, *The Defenders*, The Unit, and films: *Remember Me*, The Ringer, *Camouflage*, The Other Side Of The Wind, and *Man Of The House.*

He began his career in the 80's, working in such films as What's Love Got To Do With It, *Child's Play*, The Phantom, *El Norte*, and on JAG, *Melrose Place*, General Hospital, *The Magnificent Seven*, The X-Files, *Arli$$,* and many others.

Bo directed casting sessions for over 20 years, and has worked on farms, in the steel mills along Lake Michigan, as a newscaster for CBS affiliates, and for the U.S. Congress. He was the Coach for the Special Olympic Equestrian Team in LA for 15 years, and is a graduate of the University of Notre Dame.

Made in United States
Orlando, FL
31 January 2024

43114848R00124